Rory *Rides* Her Fake Fiancé

A BLACK CAT/GOLDEN RETRIEVER ROMCOM

BUFFED & POLISHED BOOK 2

LIZ ALDEN

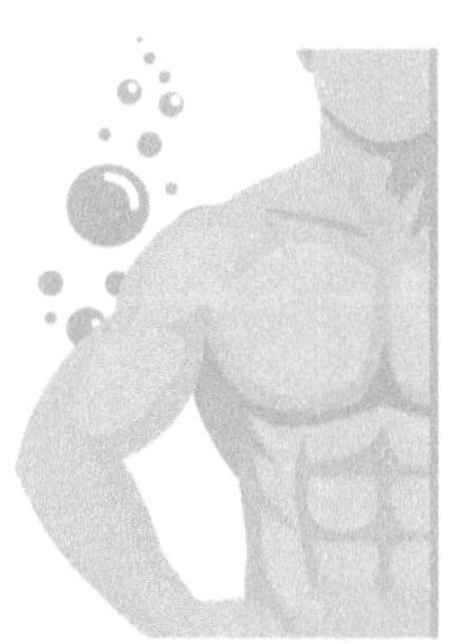 

Meet the men of Buffed & Polished, a small-town cleaning service with maximum charm and minimum clothing. This steamy romcom series features black cat/golden retriever pairings, heroes who fall first and hard, and adorable pets that will win your heart. Each book is a standalone with its own HEA.

Dear Reader, sorry I couldn't name this Fiona Fucks Her Fake Fiancé

But for real:
To my new hometown

This story contains family estrangement, grief for deceased family, parental substance abuse, and an accident resulting in hospitalization and injury.

It also includes an extremely ornery grandma who gets sick. Don't worry, she lives.
(The devil won't take her.)

Foreplay

Rory—five-foot-something of black leather, resting bitch face, and an ass so gorgeous I've cried just thinking about it—walks into my bar. She ignores the clang of the cowbell over the door and the cheers of the tipsy grannies in the corner and beelines for a stool at the counter.

"Good lord, put that away." Shielding his eyes from my megawatt smile is my best friend and boss at On the Rocks, Hunter Price. "You're gonna get someone pregnant with that thing. Maybe even me."

I ignore him and slide over to where Rory's taken a seat. Her matte-black motorcycle helmet sits on the bar next to her. "What would you like, my queen?"

Rory presses her lips together, rolling them under her teeth before answering. I'm ninety-five percent sure it's to hold back a smile. She has never once protested against my nickname for her and that's how I know she fucking loves it.

"The usual."

"So a Call of the Wild IPA, loaded tots, and my undying adoration. Got it."

I turn around and slide open the cooler, pretending to look for a bottle of the local craft beer. What I'm actually doing is watching Rory in the mirror behind the bar. Today, like every time she comes in, her long dark hair is in two braids, tucked back with a handkerchief over her head. Her lips, plush with a Cupid's bow now that they've released from her teeth, are a lush red, a contrast to her pale skin. She finishes rolling her eyes and—to my complete satisfaction—her gaze drops to my ass.

These jeans are her favorite—I wore them just for her. Not that she's admitted it. But they are my tightest ones, and in my loose scientific experiments, these are the ones that make Rory stare the most.

I quit lollygagging and pull the beer out, rip the cap off, and set it in front of Rory. Ten seconds later I've sent the order into the kitchen for the tots and I return to her, propping my chin on my fists and grinning at her.

Movement catches my eye. Hunter's getting up, shaking his head at me and rolling his eyes.

He gives me a look that roughly translates to *you are incorrigible and I love you anyway* and wanders off, probably to play pool in the back.

"So, Rory. Back in town for your spa day?"

She scoffs.

"Therapy appointment?"

"Nope." She pops the P.

I think for a minute. "Fire marshal training."

She tilts her head and narrows her eyes at me.

"I'll take that as a no. So when are you going to tell me what it is that brings you into town every other week?"

Rory doesn't live *here*, pun intended. The town of Here, New York, has roughly two thousand Herevians and Rory's not one of them. I would have bumped into her somewhere else by now. Instead, for the past two months, the only time I've seen her has been every other Sunday around 6 p.m.

"That's on a need-to-know basis," she says.

I'm honestly not sure whether that's true or she just likes keeping a secret from me.

The front door opens again, that cowbell above it clanging, and the old ladies in the back shout "I need more cowbell." Actually, it's just Janet Mullins who shouts it. The septuagenarian has a collection of pop references over the years that she can't let go of and the *SNL* skit is one of her favorites. Of course, this starts a fight with Mrs. Gardiner sitting next to her, who abhors anything the younger generations once thought was cool.

"Hey, Morgan." The cowbell ringer is Heather, a voluptuous blonde I may have hooked up with once or three times. Now she's married with a kid.

Small towns, ya know?

Still, Heather smiles at me and I give her a friendly one back. "You want a Sam Adams?" I ask.

"Nah, Collin's got one for me."

"Shout if you need more."

"Will do," she calls over her shoulder, walking toward the end of the bar where a group is gathered.

I watch her go. Collin ordered a bucket of brews, sure, but there's a big crowd down there and they might be all gone.

Heather's just about to reach Collin, to give him the

usual kiss on the cheek, when Rory says, "So, next month—"

My head whips around faster than a hunting dog hearing a whistle. "Excuse me, did you just initiate a conversation with me?"

Rory's cheeks are pink, and instead of answering she takes a swig of her beer and averts her eyes.

I put a hand to my chest. "Oh my god, why are you so obsessed with me?"

Rory chokes, coughs, and when she regains her composure, insists, "I am not obsessed with you."

"Please. You come all the way out here—"

"It's on my way—"

"—to visit our little Podunk bar."

"You carry my favorite beer."

"So does the Kinnara restaurant in town—"

"Their beer isn't cold enough."

"—and Schmidt's pool hall."

"It's full of grouchy old men!"

"You always sit right here at the bar so you can talk to me—"

"Your fake leather booths suck."

I lean against the bar to deliver my final point. "And really, Rory, you can't keep your eyes off of me."

Rory opens her mouth to argue but the cowbell rings again. I glance over and grin.

It's my other boss, Kit Hutchinson, wearing a cowboy hat. He doesn't normally come in on Sundays, since it's his busiest day of the week, but he's got a special delivery for me.

"Hey man," I say as he slides onto a barstool. I reach across the bar and we do a complicated handshake. It's mostly by rote memory now, but there's palm slapping, knuckle grinding, and pinkie wrestling.

I'd teach it to you, but it's top secret.

When we finally break, I dig out a beer for Kit and he glances over at Rory.

Then he does a double take.

"Wait, is this her?"

I lean back against the cooler and cross my arms, grinning.

"Me?" Rory's eyes widen.

"Are you Rory?"

She nods.

"Morgan talks about you all the time. When are you gonna put him out of his misery and go on a date?"

Rory turns to glare at me. I just grin wider and flex. Rory's gaze drops down. My flannel sleeves are rolled up and I'm showing off grade-A forearm porn.

I pay attention to TikTok.

"Well, I'll leave you two to your foreplay. Here." Kit stands, takes the cowboy hat off, and offers it to me. I duck down and he settles it onto my head.

"Cowboys tomorrow?"

"Cowboys tomorrow," Kit confirms. "See you at ten." He heads toward the back to see Hunter, and the two of them do our handshake, but it's the full-body version that ends in a big long hug. Like, so long it often turns into a slow dance when there's music playing. Kit's an exceptionally good hugger, and I don't think he ever pulls away first.

"Lemme guess," Rory says after I return my attention to her. Her voice has a nice low rumble that I like. The kind of voice romantics say sounds like whiskey and smoke.

Who me? You think I'm a romantic?

It's gettin' there.

"He's your BFF." She takes on a higher-pitched, mocking voice.

Aw. She's so cute.

"Since elementary school," I confirm. "Used to pass notes and play pranks and generally get into trouble together. Still do."

"Oh. Em. Gee," she deadpans. "You rebel. Serious troublemaker with that cowboy hat on."

"Hey." I lean forward, holding her gaze and pointing at the hat. "I get paid to wear this hat. Kit's my boss too."

Rory screws up her mouth and looks around. On the Rocks is the only part of Sirens Valley Lodge Ski Resort that's open all year round. "He owns this place? And I've never seen you wear a cowboy hat to bartend before."

"No. That's my other boss, Hunter, the GM of Sirens. Kit's the boss at my second job."

"What's your other job? Rodeo clown?"

"Hey, that's not a bad idea." I rub my chin. "All those masked men thirst traps on socials. I bet there are some people that have a clown kink."

Rory's eyes unfocus for a bit and then snap back to me. "What then?"

I grin. "Well, I'll give you a hint."

I walk to the end of the bar and fiddle with my phone, changing the music to something genre-appropriate.

And then, I start to take my clothes off.

There's a Fucking Snake

RORY

"Hey, Cowboy" by Devon Cole starts playing on the sound system, louder than the previous song that was cut off, but Morgan still keeps his back to me. His flannel shirt shifts and tugs against his broad shoulders, so he's clearly doing something and hiding it from my view.

I take a swig of my beer to keep myself from staring at his ass. It's a great ass—narrow waist tapering down to worn jeans. One of the pockets has a hole in the bottom.

God damn it, I'm staring. Again.

The people at the end of the bar start watching whatever Morgan's doing. This includes the really pretty white woman around our age who walked in earlier and made me irrationally jealous—seriously, all he did was smile at her. He smiles at *everyone* so why did I hate it? There's a lot of laughter and someone starts catcalling. What the hell is happening?

The chorus hits and Morgan spins around, dramatically ripping his flannel shirt open.

Holy shit.

He yanks the shirt out from his jeans and grabs the long handle of something, coming through the pass-through to this side of the bar. At this point, everyone's cheering him on, singing along to the song.

I'm already distracted by his abs. His torso is smooth and tanned, black ink up and down the side, on his chest, and a half sleeve on one shoulder. A deep V-cut draws my eyes farther south.

It doesn't help that when Devon Cole says she's a woman and not a lady, Morgan does a hip swivel that should be downright illegal.

The song moves onto the next verse and Morgan focuses on the thing in his hand—a broom—and starts sweeping toward me. When the song howls, he throws back his head and howls too, as does everyone else in the bar. Morgan has to grip the cowboy hat to keep it from falling off his head, and that makes his biceps bulge outrageously.

Why am I lightheaded?

He draws closer and I'm gripping the beer bottle so hard I'm surprised it doesn't shatter. I let go and wipe both hands on my thighs. The one that wasn't on the cool, condensed bottle is sweaty.

Morgan uses the broom like a prop, dancing with it, swaying his hips, even grinding against it, all while sweeping expertly around the legs of the barstools.

My barstool has swiveled toward Morgan of its own accord, my knees pointing to him like a compass to the

North Pole. I can't figure out where to put my eyes so they're all over the place.

Especially because I can now see the tattoos properly. There's a fucking snake running down the side of his ribs and I can practically feel the ridges under my tongue.

Oh no. This is bad. I squeeze my thighs together and try not to meet his eyes. I don't know how, but Morgan is pretty goddamned confident that I'm into him, no matter how hard I've tried not to be.

Morgan gets to my stool. He sets the broom against the bar and, with a hand on the outside of my knee that *burns* me, spins me so that my back is to the bar. He follows the movement and puts his hands on either side of me, caging me in.

That's the first time Morgan's ever touched me. Usually we have the bulky wood bar between us, which has given me so much distance from his charm—enough distance to make it easier to deflect.

And then it's all abs and hips and his cocky, far-too-confident-in-himself smile. I'm vaguely aware that the crowd has gotten louder, but Morgan's quietly singing the words and that's all I can focus on.

After what feels like too long but also not nearly long enough, Morgan pulls the hat off his head and leans back to put it between us, right over his crotch. Nothing's changed underneath. I know that. His fly is still zipped up, the black leather belt secure, but like . . . I can't *see* it and dear god, why is that hotter?

The song comes to its end. Was it always such a short song?

Morgan leans away from me, grinning, and puts his hat back on. We make eye contact and I can't help it.

I laugh.

It's a nervous laugh, a laugh that's trying to expel all

the flustered-up feelings inside of me. I'm embarrassed and turned on and don't know what I do with my hands right now so they flutter somewhere near my burning face.

Flutter. My hands *flutter.* Before today I would have told you that was impossible.

This fucking guy. The day I first walked into this bar I thought, wow, that is the friendliest bartender I've ever met. He kept looking at me and I kept ignoring him.

Er, mostly ignoring him. Have I mentioned that he's really hot? His dark blond hair is a little too long, his eyes a little too bright, his nose a little too crooked, but it all fucking works for him.

His imperfections make the whole package better.

The second time I walked into his bar, he remembered me, and his face lit up and he had a completely one-sided flirtation.

It was *good*, which is impressive considering I didn't give him any ammunition.

The third time it was all over. The way he greeted me, you'd have thought I was a long-lost friend. Well, maybe not—we didn't do the handshake he did with that other guy, but it was so familiar.

So nice to have someone happy to see me.

Morgan is standing stock-still in front of me and I'm still smiling, coming down off that embarrassing laugh.

But when I look up at him, all the humor drains out of me. He's *staring*, the wide smile eroded to one side of his mouth. The teasing light is fading, the flirtiness disappearing.

I press my lips together. God damn it.

I look away before I can see the transformation end in sympathy . . . or worse.

The crowd is still loud, cheering, and I feel Morgan behind me shaking off what he saw. I sip my beer, and on my periphery, his hand reaches out to grab the broom handle.

"Look at all this shit," he shouts over the cheering. In the mirror I watch as he raises his arms. "I swept this morning, you filthy animals. Kit, grab me the dustpan."

In the reflection, Morgan sweeps along the floor, teasingly shoving people out of the way while his friend—white guy, floppy hair, rangier than Morgan—grabs the cleaning supplies and they work together, ducking down out of sight.

"Like a professional," someone says in a lilting voice, and a few people chuckle.

The crowd resumes its normal hum, the music gets turned down, and after a few minutes, Morgan appears in front of me again, still shirtless.

"So you're a stripper," I say.

"Nope." He grins. "I didn't take my clothes off."

"You took your shirt off," I point out.

He puts his hand over his chest, his thumb resting against a thick black line that slopes down over his pec. "I'm so glad you noticed. But that was the setup."

"You danced."

"The dance was for you. I may have gotten carried away." He grins, unrepentant. "I don't dance that way for *anyone*, you know."

I shake my head. I don't think he's lying to me, per se, but that sure felt like I was minutes away from getting a lap dance. And what else could the hint have been?

Someone calls for more drinks, and Morgan trots off to take care of them. He returns a few minutes later, dropping my loaded tater tots off in front of me with a fresh beer, and then I try to ignore him milling around while he lets me eat in peace.

I'm about halfway done when someone comes up to

the bar a few seats down from me. Most of the bar patrons are either in the booths behind me or at the far end by the pool table where Morgan's friend Kit is playing a game with the guy who was sitting here when I first arrived.

This person, though, isn't a twenty- or thirty-something local that fits right into this little dive bar. She's an older white woman, maybe in her sixties, with a silver-gray bob and a color-coordinated outfit, complete with a jeweled brooch.

She holds a martini glass, which, in my entire two months coming here, I've never seen one before.

Morgan spots her and saunters over, full, charming grin in place.

"Mrs. Gardiner, ready for another martini?"

She sniffs. "Morgan, my glass has been empty for nearly a half hour."

I'm sure that's not true, because I haven't even been here a half hour.

Morgan is nonplussed by her tone. "Sorry, Mrs. Gardiner. It's hard to see it over that bucket of beer at the table."

"Or you've been too busy trying to charm your way into this woman's pants." She says it with something that could be a sneer.

"Your lips to God's ears," he says, flicking his eyes at me with a tease. Is he just so charming he can't help himself?

The lady gasps. "Morgan. What would your grand-mother think, you cavorting all over the place with your shirt off? Or your boss? I have half a mind to report you."

"He's right over there. You know Hunter. He took your granddaughter to prom, remember?"

"I'm talking about the Schaefers," she snaps. "I don't

know what they're thinking, leaving you two to run this place. You'll run it into the ground!"

Morgan's smile doesn't slip, but I swear the muscle in his cheek jumps. "Why don't you head on back to your booth with your friends and I'll whip up that drink for you and bring it over? That way you can leave my future bride to enjoy her own drink in peace."

I roll my eyes. This isn't the first time that Morgan has joked about marrying me. In fact, the second time I was in his bar, he asked how the tots were, and I stared him dead in the eye and said, "It's fried potatoes."

He'd put his hand to his chest, staggering. "Oh baby, I love the way you pay me compliments. Will you marry me?"

I'd scoffed, he'd laughed, and it had been enough encouragement for him to keep it up.

Mrs. Gardiner sniffs. "Be sure that you do, Morgan. I'm not your mother who'll let you get away with far too much."

Morgan turns away from me so I can't see his reaction to that, but it's a pretty obvious dismissal. The rude lady harrumphs, but follows his advice and goes back to her friends.

I watch them while Morgan mixes the drink. There are two older women at the table she joins. While Mrs. Gardiner is dressed pretty nicely in her pantsuit, the other two are more casual. One, a white woman with a short halo of curls wears a shirt that says "Shuck the Patriarchy" with a row of oysters below it, and the other, a dark-skinned woman, has long gray dreads hanging over her shoulder and an outfit with bright colors and a flowy, hippie vibe.

These women are about my grandmother's age, and I wonder where they live. It's a small town. I bet they have families nearby that take care of them, not put them in a home like I've done.

I shake the guilt away and eat the last tater tot. This is why I always come here—I need a buffer between my own grandmother and the real world.

"For the record," Morgan says as he mixes the drink. "I'm not just trying to get into your pants."

I raise an eyebrow. Whatever he's going to say is bound to be outrageous, and he doesn't mean it. Despite all his words, today is the first time Morgan's ever crossed the figurative bar with me. He's teased and flirted plenty, but Morgan isn't interested that way, especially after seeing his reaction to my teeth.

We both wait while he shakes up the martini. He pops the top and pours it into a chilled glass.

"No, I'm trying to give you a night that forever changes the way you dream. The kind of night that leaves you shaky and wrung out and thinking about me, that small-town bartender that gave you the ride of your life."

And with that, he picks up the filled martini glass and saunters off.

Most Beautiful Princess

Morgan

I hum along to the Garth Brooks song as I wash the dishes. I dance a bit as I go—not technically part of the job description, but this is just for me anyway. Mrs. Donner, this morning's client who requested the cowboy-themed package, is asleep in the living room.

She slipped off about five minutes after Kit and I got started. I kept an eye on her since Kit is back in her bathroom cleaning, and after a few minutes I gently took the whiskey sour out of her hand and set it on the side table.

It's not uncommon for her to fall asleep. She's in her late eighties, and while she's a fun lady, apparently the pull of sleep is too strong to counter the thrill of having two young, shirtless men clean your house.

Kit comes out from the back rooms with two small

bags of trash to take out. He glances at the sleeping woman and grins.

We're both wearing pretty much the same outfit as I was wearing last night when I showed off to Rory: a cowboy hat and worn jeans (although not the tight ones Rory likes). I've traded my belt for something a little showier and switched my comfortable bar shoes for work boots.

We're both shirtless. We're shirtless for every job.

Kit's business, Buffed & Polished, started as a side hustle and it's blown up. It's a great side hustle for me, Hunter, and Silas. I've known these guys pretty much my whole life, so we make a good team. I pick up a few gigs when I'm not at the bar in the off-season and Hunter does the same. Ski season is too busy to do much, which is when Silas picks up the slack.

Mrs. Donner bought the Whiskey Sour package, but we've also got a Cosmopolitan (bow ties and the titular cocktail), a Teacher (fake glasses and the lesser-known gin cocktail), and the Fireman (cheap Halloween costume fireman pants and a Fireball whisky cocktail that I personally think is disgusting). I keep telling Kit we should do a Masked Men— or a Regency-themed one, but he just says I need to get off TikTok and stop watching *Bridgerton*.

I guess our off-season clientele is a bit older and probably not as up with the trends. But during ski season, we get parties coming up from the city, and Kit's got a friend who swears her book club about two hours away would hire him.

"Done with the bathroom," Kit says in a low voice. He sets the trash bags by our cart and then makes a few trips back and forth to put the cleaning supplies away. I finish the dishes, check Mrs. Donner's fridge for moldy food, and then run a mop over the linoleum.

Mrs. Donner's daughter hires us to come in once a month and deep clean. I think it's mostly just for fun though, since the place always looks pretty good.

And since there's not much to clean, I can think about Rory. Last night after she finished her tater tots she was subdued. I know she enjoyed the show—her eyes were so big and they darted all over my body like she couldn't figure out what part of me she liked the best.

Personally, I think it was the snake tattoo. I got it to remind me not to turn my back on a viper, but if she likes it, I'll show it off.

As she does every time she comes, she moved to a booth once she was done with her beer, read on her phone, and drank water for about an hour before she left.

She doesn't even say goodbye to me, her roaring motorcycle alerting me as she pulls away.

One of these days I'm going to win her over. She'll linger longer, waiting for me to close. Maybe we won't even make it home—maybe I'll get to have her right there in the bar, her legs wrapped around me, her black pants dangling from one ankle while I thrust inside of her.

And then, of course, we'd do it all over again in bed when I get her back to my place.

Dammit. Now I'm sporting a boner on the job. I turn my mind back to cleaning before Mrs. Donner wakes up and I give her a heart attack.

Kit and I finish up our chores and he crouches down next to Mrs. Donner in the armchair. He places a gentle hand on her arm and whispers her name.

Her eyes open and she blinks up at Kit. "Oh," she says, her voice rough from sleep. "Did I fall asleep again?"

Kit grins and takes her proffered hand, helping her sit up and then stand. "Yes, ma'am, you did."

"Well, fiddlesticks. I didn't even get to enjoy the show you boys put on."

"Don't worry," Kit says with a wink. "I enjoyed it enough for the both of us."

She laughs and pats his chest, right over where he has the tattoo that goes with mine. She may squeeze a little, but Kit doesn't say anything.

Sometimes we have to get strict about our no-touching policy, especially in the case of the bachelorette parties, but Mrs. Donner's harmless.

She grabs her purse and walks us to the door, rooting around for her pocketbook. She gives us two twenties each, and we thank her, hamming it up by adding a drawl to our "Thank you, ma'am," and tipping our hats to her.

Kit and I grab all the supplies and load the van. The side of the old Dodge used to advertise Kit's other company—Hutchinson & Co Cleaning—but the new lettering has the Buffed & Polished logo in bold colors and a stylized set of abs on the doors.

"You got more to do today?" I ask.

"Yup. A cabin at my parents' and one of the Airbnbs in town."

Hutchinson & Co is a regular cleaning service. He's the only one in town, and his parents own a few rental properties, which is how he started. Sometimes he cleans for the lodge too, but those jobs are few and far between in the off-season.

"Lunch?" I suggest as we slide into the front seat, picking up our T-shirts before I sit. It's one of the hottest days of the year today, and my skin is warm from the sun beating down while we worked in the driveway.

"Hell yeah." We spend a minute putting our shirts back on before he starts the engine and we head into town.

I check my phone. There's a missed call from my uncle,

which is weird. I'll return the call later. I clear the rest of the notifications—social media and junk mail—and focus back on Kit.

He gossips about his family, complaining about his sister who still lives with his parents. She's in her late twenties and I love to tease Kit about how he's thirty-two and also still living with his parents.

"It's in the basement," he insists. "That's different."

We drive past the old mill building with its For Sale sign. I have no idea who's going to buy a fifty-thousand-square-foot building that hasn't been used in so long that people can't even remember what it used to mill. But it's pretty close to town, and therefore a big eyesore.

Here, New York, is a sleepy little place when it's warmer. There are only a few options open for lunch, and we pick Sweet Persuasions, the coffee shop and bakery. We sit outside, since it's a sunny day, and pick up our sandwiches. Mine is grilled veggies and mozzarella, served on a toasted baguette. Yum.

"How's the bar fund coming?" Kit asks.

All the money I earn from this side gig goes into my Buy Your Own Bar Someday Soon fund. That's literally the name of the bank account online. I'm dedicated as fuck. Even the twenty in my pocket will go in.

It's not that I don't like working for Hunter at Sirens. But the Schaefers who own the lodge have pretty much checked out. Hunter and I brainstorm ways to bring more business in and the Schaefers, who claim that we have autonomy, slap us down. Usually, it's after we've already announced the event or special or whatever it is that we're trying to push. Hunter and I have a hunch that they only know what's going on because they see it on Instagram instead of reading the emails we cc them into. So sometimes we just . . . throw secret parties.

Not ideal, I know.

I'd love to have a bar of my own. Maybe walking distance from the house I rent. Some place I could bring my golden, Princess, to work with me, some place that is busy every day, not just in ski season or Sunday night when there's half-price happy hour. There's enough business in the winter for another bar . . . if you can survive through the summer.

"Eh." I shrug. "Slow but steady."

We talk about the local real estate. Silas, who's a part-time agent, messages me anytime something comes on the market. The problem is that in a town this size, there's only a few places that are already kitted out as bars. One of those is sitting right across the street, but the guy who owns it is asking a ridiculous price. I don't know why—he doesn't need the money. He owns several properties and businesses in town, like the one the dispensary rents and the old theater. About half of them are shuttered and listed for bonkers prices.

The locations in my price range all need work—bars built, bathrooms upgraded, and in one case, squatters kicked out. I don't have the money to do the first two or the heart to do the last one. Winters are tough up here.

Leo, who works in construction, tells me he'd do the work for free in exchange for a partial ownership. Silas, when he's not working as a real estate agent (in a town this size, I'm sure if you added up all of the work the agents have, it wouldn't even amount to a full-time job), is also a photographer. He takes pictures of our drink specials at Sirens and would do the same for me in exchange for free drinks. And Kit's got his cleaning services to offer.

Even with all that free labor and the love that comes with it, I still need a lot more money if I'm ever going to afford a place.

"You'll get there," Kit says, always the optimist.

"Maybe by the time I'm forty."

"You could quit the bar and work more for me," he teases. We both know I wouldn't do that to Hunter.

"You need to import some workers," I tell him. "If you're ever going to buy your own place, that is. Don't you have some friends in Fork Lick you can recruit? Get them to come up for a weekend and do a few jobs."

Kit snorts. "You've met Alex. If I *could* tear him away from his farm and Molly for the weekend, do you think I could get him to strip down and clean?"

"Touché." Kit's college roommate is a big, burly farmer who makes up for Kit's blabbermouth with his stoic silence. "With that beard he'd do a great mountain man theme."

We shoot ideas for a mountain man package that'll never happen as we finish up lunch and leave. Kit and I are both scruffy, so we float the idea of growing thick beards and offering a limited-time special. I hate growing a beard—it's itchy—but I'd do it for Kit.

It's a Monday and the bar's closed, so Kit takes me home, just a few blocks away. I could have walked, but I know what Kit wants.

The minute I open my front door he's down on the floor with Princess, who whines and moans uncontrollably, her favorite hard rubber bone in her mouth and her lips pulled back and eyes squinty.

"Who's the most beautiful Princess in the world?" Kit asks my golden retriever. I swear her answering whine sounds like "Meeeeeeeeeeee!"

I toe my shoes off and rest my keys and wallet on the table by the door. My house is cozy, but it works for me and Princess. Two bedrooms, a shared bath, and a fenced-in yard that's a smidge too small for a rambunctious golden, but we make it work. It's one block off the main road and the smallest house in the neighborhood. The best part is that there's a teenaged girl next door who loves to come play with Princess on nights that I have to work.

I grab myself a soda from the fridge and plop myself down on the couch in view of Princess with the only man she loves as much as she loves me.

Since Kit lives with his parents, he can't get a dog yet. They have an orange tabby with one brain cell and a hatred of other animals. Honestly, you'd think a cat that was so dumb he regularly attacks his own tail so bad he cries out in pain would be ambivalent about other pets, but I guess that one brain cell is dumb and angry.

Maybe he's angry about being dumb.

Kit finally comes up for air. "Princess, my darling, my love, my soulmate. You wanna come with me back to work?"

He says it with an upticked tone, the same one I would use to say we're going for a walk, and her whole body rockets up. She drops the bone and spins in circles, pausing occasionally to look at me and then the leash hanging on the wall.

"Don't be an asshole," I tell Kit.

He laughs. "You know you're going to take her for a walk next. I just love to see her all riled up."

She's only been alone for three hours, but yes, I will take her out for a walk next, so I get to my feet as Kit clips the leash on. We walk outside and Kit waits for Princess to pee. My dog squats and also lifts a leg like a weirdo, but does her business and then smothers Kit with kisses before he says goodbye and drives off.

I head down the street with Princess and let her sniff whatever she wants. She played in the backyard this morning and I'll probably spend the afternoon back there with her again trying to wear her out. Since Mondays are my only day off from the bar, I enjoy my time with her as much as I can.

A motorcycle roars from somewhere nearby, going down Main Street, probably. I can't see it but I hear it. It's different from Rory's, but it makes me think of her anyway.

Why does she come to town every other week? Where does she go after she leaves my bar and why do I never see her around?

Too many questions and too few answers.

Their Boyfriends
Are Ancient

Rory

"I'm moving," Grandma says while we walk down the hall together. Well, she hobbles down the hall with her cane at a really fast clip, and I lengthen my stride to keep up. We've just left her apartment in the senior living community and are headed downstairs to have lunch.

"You're not moving."

"I hate it here."

"You promised me six months. It's only been two. You haven't even given it a chance."

"Bah. What's there to give a chance? All the women here hate me. They think I'm trying to steal their boyfriends."

"Well, are you?" Grandma may be eighty-three years old but I wouldn't put it past her.

We arrive at the elevator and Grandma presses the button to call it.

"Hell no," she says. "Their boyfriends are ancient. If I'm going to spend my time with a man he better be a hot young thing."

The elevator doors open and Grandma steps in, joining an old man with a walker who was already in the elevator. He blinks at us. It's a walker with the tennis balls on the bottom, although this is a really nice place. If someone can afford to live here, they can afford the fancy walkers with the sliding feet.

Grandma aggressively pushes the first-floor button, even though it's already lit. "At my age, the next time I have sex might be the last. Who wants to waste it on an old fart like this one?" She jabs her cane in the direction of the old man.

If the old man takes offense to this—if he even hears her—she doesn't give him a chance to object. "No, if I'm going out with a bang, I'm going out with someone at least twenty years my junior. A nice young stallion. Like the one you should have."

I roll my eyes, not even bothering to hide it from Grandma. She should check her math—twenty years her junior is sixty-three, and I'm pretty sure if I brought a sixty-three-year-old man to meet Grandma she'd be pissed about the age gap and then complain that I'm "hogging the eligible men."

"I hear," she says, leaning toward me, "that there are strippers in Here that make house calls."

My mind flashes to Morgan and all the abs and obliques and tattoos that I saw two weeks ago, and I squeeze my eyes shut extra hard. Grandma's trying to distract me. I do not for one minute believe that in a small town like Here there are male strippers that cater to a geri-atric audience.

"You can't just randomly flit about to different places."

"Why not? You're flitting about too."

"I'm not flitting. There's no flitting."

Grandma looks at me out of the corner of her eye. "It would be different if you were settled down."

I ignore that comment. I'm aware that if I was in any kind of committed relationship, Grandma would stay settled. She would complain constantly, but she wouldn't be making me pack up her shit every few months.

It's one of the only regrets I have about my last breakup.

"You're not moving," I tell Grandma. "You have four more months. You need to make friends."

"Why should I make friends?" Grandma huffs. "You haven't made any either."

The elevator dings and Grandma's off like a shot and around the corner. I politely hold the door open for the old man, though I refuse to make eye contact with him. He really didn't need to overhear my grandma's death-sex wish.

He shuffles out. "My name is Arthur Hayes." He speaks glacially and has a slight tremble in his hand when he raises it up to point after my grandmother. "You can tell her to find me at apartment number one-four—"

"Yeah, okay, thanks, Gramps."

I drop my arm and chase after my grandmother. The old man is mostly out the door, he'll be fine.

When I come around the corner she's waiting for me halfway down to the cafe. "Hurry up, the clock is ticking."

"Lunch isn't over until two," I shoot back, catching up to her.

"I wasn't talking about lunch, I was talking about my life."

"Four more months, Grandma. Make some friends."

"*You* make friends." She says it like a threat, which, well . . . it is. This is Grandma's fourth retirement community. The first one only lasted a month, but when she moved from the second one, I caught on to her game. She's going to princess-and-the-pea her way through all the retirement communities in the tristate area, wasting her money and both our time until I agree to quit my job and stay home with her.

As it is, I'm on the road too much to live with her properly, but she can't live by herself. Who knows what mayhem she could get up to on her own. Once I came to visit her and found a miniature pony living in the house with her. In the house!

"I do have friends," I insist.

She scoffs. "Liar."

We get to the cafe and my grandmother greets the hostess by reminding her she doesn't like to sit next to the windows because they're too drafty.

The hostess just smiles. This must be one of the ones Grandma hasn't broken yet.

We're led to a table by the wall and settle in with the menu, not that I need one. The food is pretty good here, and I've got a favorite meal picked out. But Grandma studies the menu as if she's never seen it before, when I happened to know for a fact that they slip one under her door every morning. There are several regular dishes and a few daily specials.

I look around the room while Grandma gives commentary on the menu. "Liver and onions! How old do they think we are?" and "Quinoa? I'm not a hippie." There's a group of women my grandma's age sitting in the corner.

"What about her?" I nod my head toward the woman I recognize from the last time I was here. "You could make friends with her."

Grandma peers in that direction and huffs. "She told me I had poor taste in music."

I roll my eyes again. Honestly, between her and Morgan it's a miracle that I don't strain something. If one can even strain their eyeballs, I'm sure these two would drive me to it. "You can't honestly tell me you thought this crowd would like your EDM playlist."

"It makes me feel young." She turns back to her menu and puts it down decisively. "I'm going to have the salmon. Now, who is it?"

I turn back to the woman. "I don't know her name." She looks like a Betty, if I had to guess.

"No." Grandma rolls her eyes. See where I get it from? "Who's your friend in Here?"

Oh. Uh-oh. Grandma's fact checking.

Well, I do, technically, maybe, kind of, sort of have one friend here. "Morgan."

Grandma stares at me, and then makes a rolling motion with her hand. "Morgan . . . ?"

I do not know his last name. "Morgan the bartender."

She harrumphs. "Morgan. Are *they* a potential love interest?"

Grandma may be a pain in my ass, but she is a strong ally. Ever since I came out to her as bisexual—and explained gender fluidity to her—she's always been careful with pronouns.

"Morgan is a he."

"You didn't answer my question. Is he hot?"

"He's too young for you, Grandma."

"I didn't know there was a limit. What is it? Twenty-five?"

I put my face in my hands. "Jesus."

"They need to be that young if they're going to keep up with me."

"In the hallway or in the bedroom?" I mutter, thinking about Grandma power walking the halls.

"Both." There is nothing wrong with my grandma's hearing, even though sometimes I wish there was. "And obviously he's hot, or you wouldn't be blushing."

"I am not blushing!"

"Has he not asked you out yet?"

I pause and think about it. Does teasing me about sex count? Probably not, but maybe if I had *prospects* in this town, Grandma might actually try. "He has."

"Of course he asked you out, he's not blind." Grandma gestures at me. "Wait, is he blind?"

"No."

"So you said no."

"I said no."

"Why not? Too hot for you?" She looks over her glasses at me. "Is he poor? You know that doesn't matter. You could use a good house husband."

"I said no because—"

"Because you think you should die old and alone just like me."

Thankfully, we're interrupted by the server coming to take our order. This one's a blond woman, who greets us in a singsong voice and repeats our order back to us as if we've ordered the *best thing ever!*

(Trust me, there was an exclamation point.)

Grandma asks approximately fifty questions about the menu. Most of them are about the regular menu items, so I know she's just testing the waitress, who starts to shift and gives me wide eyes, searching for a rescue. I throw her a bone and ask for a few more minutes.

When the waitress leaves, Grandma eyes me. She holds the silence too long and there is about a sixty-forty split between her ragging on me more or her changing the subject to complain about the housing situation again.

I cross my arms and rest my elbows on the table, bracing myself for what she's going to dish out next.

But then her face shifts and oh no. I forgot about the other part. It's not a sixty-forty split. It's maybe a 58-38-4 split. There's a four percent chance I'm going to be reminded of why I love this woman so much.

"Rory," she says gently.

Yup, the four percent is making an appearance despite all odds.

"You don't like to think about it, and I get that. You've thought about death too much in your life."

I look away. It's not often that either of us bring up the car accident anymore.

"But someday I will die. Probably soon. Maybe not." She shrugs. "But probably. And I just want you to be happy."

"I know, Grandma."

She reaches over and pats my hand twice, and then grips it. I look at her, and we smile at each other. I'm lucky to have had such a strong, fun woman raise me. It's not every grandparent that can look after a ten-year-old.

"Besides . . ." She releases my hand and pats it again. "You need to get laid."

Fifty Percent

Rory

After lunch, we get pedicures in the salon in the community building, and then we go upstairs to her apartment and I help her pay some bills because she refuses to use autopay.

Grandma's black cat, Bartholomeow, makes an appearance just in time to sit on the papers I'm trying to read and hiss at me.

At five thirty I drop Grandma off at the nicer restaurant in the building and make the drive over to Morgan's bar. I'll be back in a couple hours to stay the night, but Grandma and I need a break after spending all day with each other.

Plus, when the residents show up to dinner alone, they seat all the singles at a big table. I always hope this ends in a friendship, but Grandma said there's a new couple who've moved into the community on the lower age range and she's hoping to get in good with them on the off chance the wife dies.

Which sounded more like a threat than I'd like to think about.

I pull open the door to On the Rocks and walk inside. I get about halfway to the bar before I realize that something's wrong.

Something's really wrong.

It's quieter, for one. People are huddled together talking in low whispers. The music's too mellow for the vibe Morgan usually goes for.

But also, Morgan's not front and center. It takes me a moment to find him talking to a couple of people down the bar. Like he can feel my gaze, he looks up and . . .

Oh no. That smile is about fifty percent of what it usually is.

Who died?

Morgan leaves his friends and meets me at my seat, grabbing a bottle of Call of the Wild on the way.

"What's going on?"

Morgan sighs and runs his hand through his hair.

He's not even going to tease me about starting a conversation? Or call me his queen?

Instead, Morgan leans his elbows against the bar. "It was just announced this morning that the owners are gonna sell the lodge."

My brows come together. "Not Hunter?"

"No, he's the GM. The Schaefers are the owners and he runs it when they aren't here."

I lean forward, ignoring my beer.

"So someone else will be the boss? Will you lose your job?"

Morgan blows out his breath. Since we're both leaning

onto the bar, this might be the closest I've ever been to his eyes, which are a sky blue.

Except for last time. But I wasn't making eye contact last time.

"It's more than that," he tells me. "This town has been struggling for some time now. The lodge brings good business in the winter, but a few years ago they shut down their adventure park, and summers dried right up."

"But couldn't someone else buy the lodge?"

He grimaces. "There are a few options and none of them are good. There's this guy, Joseph Rance, who likes to buy up property and sit on it. Half the unused buildings in town are empty because of him. Who knows if he'd actually want to run things. Then there's also one of the ski conglomerates up here. It's not Vail, but who knows what changes they'd make."

He breaks eye contact, looking around the room. "They'd probably shut the bar down to renovate, and it'd be easier to fire me than keep me on. Then they'd want someone with actual food and beverage experience, which I don't have, other than this place."

When his eyes come back to mine, they're duller, missing that twinkle I associate with Morgan.

"That sucks." Ugh. That's something you tell people when they get stuck in traffic or something, not when their livelihood—the whole town's livelihood—is in jeopardy.

He snorts. "Yeah it does suck. Because you know what? You belong here." Morgan straightens, holding his arms out wide.

I roll my eyes, even though it doesn't sound like a line. But line or not, it makes my heart flutter with the way he says it.

"I'm serious," he continues. "That's our town motto. You Belong *Here*. We may not be a happening place, and we've got our problems, but we live our motto. Everyone is welcome here. Especially you." He winds down, settling his forearms on the worn wood of the bar.

I belong where my grandmother is, I tell myself firmly. I do not belong in Here, New York. Not with a dying town, not with a grandma who has no friends, and definitely not with a charming bartender.

Power Hungry

Morgan

Hunter is being secretive. He made a new group text with a bunch of us, titled it Super Secret Meeting, and suggested we meet up at my place—most likely so everyone could play with Princess—but won't tell us why. He's in my living room now, leaning against the wall. There are eight of us here, my closest friends. These are people I see almost every day, people I've grown up with.

Herevians.

We're just waiting on Kit. Hunter's anxious, though. I've known him since first grade, and he's peeling the label off his beer and barely listening to the conversation.

It's Monday, so the bar is closed. It's also the week between visits from Rory. Last week, she didn't even have a second beer, she just ate her tots, drank the one beer, and left early.

Who can blame her? I wasn't any fun to be around and, as much as Rory pretends, she likes the flirty, fun me.

And I just wasn't in the mood last week.

Silas and Bailey, the only couple, are sharing the over-sized armchair. Silas is a white guy with a hipster vibe—complete with the glasses. Bailey, Hunter's sister, is curvy and has chestnut hair and freckles that are fading into her pale skin since summer's over. Tuan, whose family is Vietnamese and owns the best restaurant in town, shares the love seat with me, running his hand over his closely cropped hair. Jared, a scruffy, dark-haired white dude and heir to the Golden Voice Brewery, perches on the arm next to me, his daughter at her grandmother's house. Quinn, a lithe blond woman and the town's best electrician, had pulled in a kitchen chair and is sitting on it backward.

Princess is on the couch in Leo's and Jared's laps. They're talking about Leo's latest construction project, each with a hand on Princess's belly. She's in doggy heaven. They've saved room for Kit, because they know wherever Kit sits is where Princess will be, and the couch is the only piece of furniture big enough for people and a seventy-pound dog.

At least, she *was* in doggy heaven. Princess gets up off the couch and darts to the window so fast that if you'd blinked, you'd have missed it. She knocks Leo's beer over, and it's on the couch and in his lap, so there's a kerfuffle of cleaning up while my dog stares out the window, tail wagging once, then stopping, then wagging once again, and stopping again.

Then I hear a car door slam and I know Kit's arrived. Princess knows too, and she goes bananas, barking and jumping and whining.

I swear she's well behaved for me. Kit just brings something out of her.

Probably because he lets her do whatever the fuck she wants. As soon as he comes in the door, she's all over him. "Princess," he laughs while she pogos up to try to lick his face. "Down, girl."

He has no authority, so she ignores him, and I leave Kit to manage the trouble he inspires. By the time we get Leo and Jared cleaned up and Princess calmed down, Hunter's pacing, too strung out to sit anymore, apparently.

"Okay." He sets his bottle down. "I have a proposal for you all."

"You're a handsome man but I'm not marrying you," Kit jokes.

Hunter rolls his eyes.

"I have an idea. It's not a plan yet, but it could be. I just thought we should talk about it first. But I feel really good about this. I'm totally certain that between all of us, we can figure this out. It'll take a lot of work. But we're good at that. Morgan, you've always wanted your own bar. And Kit, your parents have already invested so much into this town. And Leo—"

"Leo's wondering what the hell you're talking about," Leo says.

"Right." Hunter makes a rewinding motion with his hands. "We should buy Sirens Valley Lodge."

There's a moment of silence, and then Jared growls, "Fuck. Off."

Kit laughs. Hard. Tuan and I make eye contact and chuckle. Bailey and Silas are quiet, but Bailey watches us all with wide eyes. I've known her since she was a kid too —as Hunter's older sister, she was always on the outskirts of our group. But a few months ago she moved back to Here to be with Silas, occasionally driving into the city for work.

"I don't get the joke," Leo complains.

"It's not a joke. I think we should buy Sirens Valley Lodge."

Kit's still laughing, but it's tinged with hysteria now. "How the hell do you think we can do that?"

Hunter holds up his hands. "Okay, think about it——"

"We are," Leo says.

"I mean for more than thirty seconds." He holds out a finger. "The property is for sale but the closing won't happen until April, the end of the ski season."

"How do you know that?" Quinn asks.

"I talked to Meredith about it." Meredith's one of the other real estate agents in the area. She's Silas's main competition, but like him, it's only one of her jobs.

Hunter holds up another finger. "That gives us time to save up and apply for loans. If we can get a bank loan, we probably only need twenty percent or so of the deposit. We may even be able to talk the Schaefers into self-financing."

"Okay, but twenty percent is still . . ." Leo trails off.

Hunter opens up his phone. He doesn't type anything, but he reads the number off. I bet he's got a spreadsheet started already.

"That's a lot of money," Leo says faintly.

It is a lot of money. Money none of us have, except maybe Hunter, though he hasn't actually said if he has enough. Bailey might have the money too . . . she works for a firm in the city—New York, that is—as some kind of manager . . . in renewable energy, maybe?

"Split nine ways with all of us in the room," Hunter points out. "Or more if we invite other people to buy in. It's not *that* much." He gestures to me. "Morgan's already saving for his own bar. Well, you could buy the bar you already work in." He gestures widely at the room. "I already have some money in the bank. Kit's saving up for a house. Now I'm not saying he has to spend it on the lodge, obviously, but it's an option, right?"

"I *will* be saving up for a house someday," Kit interjects. "I've only been in business two years. I'm barely profitable, living at my parents' and trying to pay back the money they lent me to start."

"Okay, well. Leo? Silas? Quinn? I'm sure you all have a bit of savings." Hunter's shoulders are sagging under the weight of our objections.

"Uh, no," Leo says. "I don't have"—he counts on his fingers—"five figures of extra spending money lying around."

Silas rubs his hands over his face. "I work three jobs, man, and I'm saving . . . I'm saving up for some renovations. Do you think I have a ton of money?"

Close one, Silas. We all know he's saving for an engagement ring.

Bailey squeezes his bicep, concern etching her brow.

Hunter gentles his voice. "I know you work three jobs." He peers at his notes. "Another option is that you can contribute work instead. So Silas, you could use your buyer's commission toward your stake. Leo, Morgan, and Quinn, you could donate your labor. Kit, Jared, and Bailey . . . I'm not sure about you yet, but we can work on that."

"But . . ." Leo scratches his head. "How is that paying the Schaefers?"

"It's not. We'd have to figure that out. But hang on. I have more ideas." He scrolls down on his phone. "We can hold a fundraiser. It could be beforehand, but I think after closing would be better, because then we could use the property and have the fundraiser onsite. People love meat raffles."

He looks up at us, and we don't say anything. He

consults his phone again. "We could structure the lodge like a co-op."

"What's a co-op?" Leo asks.

"It's like REI," I say. But, just because I have a membership at the outdoor supply chain doesn't mean I understand how it works.

Kit snaps his fingers. "Alex's farm is part of a dairy co-op. But I don't think it's that great for him?"

"I've only done some cursory research," Hunter says. "But there's a few places we could use as examples. They are really popular with local grocery stores—there's one in Albany—and, of course, REI. I'd have to consult with a lawyer, but it means people buy ownership of the lodge."

"Who?" Leo asks.

"Anyone. We would incentivize it. A lifetime membership of . . . I don't know . . . five hundred dollars? It gets you twenty-five percent off lift tickets for life, or invitations to owners-only events or something."

"It's a way to quickly raise cash, I guess," I muse. As to raising my own up-front money, there is one thing I could do. I've been putting it off because it sucks, but . . .

"Yes!" Hunter grabs on to the positive thought. "I'm sure if we put our heads together we could come up with a solid plan and find the money. We could be partners. Plus!" He's really gearing up now. "Think about it. This is an opportunity for us to shape the town. We're the next generation of Herevians." He drops his phone on the armchair and plants his hands on his chest, looking each of us in the eye. "Think of every time the town has done something we hated. Like when they vetoed that food truck festival Tuan planned. Or when the old-timers voted against Picture Main Street to make downtown prettier and more functional. And we could get the adventure park back open again, bringing more business into the town in the off-season."

"How would we do all that?" This is from a completely bewildered Leo.

"I'm not saying that we'd instantly have the power to do it. But we would have influence in the town. We could hold events of our own, support the community in ways we haven't even dreamed of because we simply haven't thought of them yet. We could hold a Pride festival in June, expand the summer programs for kids, host the food trucks on our own property . . . Tuan, you've been wanting to get a food truck."

Tuan twists his mouth to the side. "We're always running on fumes in the fall before business picks up in the winter. And I can't afford both a food truck *and* the lodge. I can't even afford the food truck yet, and that's less."

"Okay," Hunter continues, not deterred enough, IMHO. "The point is . . . we could do *whatever we want.*"

Kit laughs nervously. "Okay, someone's getting power hungry already."

"Why not? *Why not?*"

No one says anything for a few long moments.

"Let us think about it," I hedge. "You're asking a lot and I should look into some things." Some things like a debt owed. But still, if I add what my brother owes me to my savings, I'm only halfway there. There's no way we can get the money together.

"It's not a no," Silas says. "But it's a big risk. I have to think about it."

"That's all I ask for now," Hunter promises. "Just think it over."

The Biggest Fucking Diamond

Morgan

Hunter's proposal niggles my mind all the next day, which is ridiculous. What is there to think about? I don't have the money. Even if I did somehow have the money, I doubt any of the rest of the guys are going to be able to dredge up enough.

Or at least, that's what I thought. But Wednesday morning, a few hours before I meet my uncle for lunch, I get a text in the new group chat.

SAVE SIRENS VALLEY LODGE

SILAS

Bailey and I are in.

I'm surprised, obviously. But good for them. And yes,

Hunter changed the group chat name after our meeting. He's enthusiastic.

Okay, so that makes three people. Still doesn't mean the rest of us are gonna find the money.

It does encourage me to think more about trekking out to my brother's place. I just have to find the time between working both jobs.

On the walk to Main Street, I shift my attention to Uncle Robert. He's my mom's only sibling, and if you knew my mom, you'd be wary. But that's just Mom. I've only met Uncle Robert a few times and he seems nice. I follow his two daughters on Instagram and they post wholesome family stuff, the likes of which my mom and my brother don't even aspire to.

The last time I saw him was at my grandmother's funeral last year. Just like my uncle, I didn't know Grandma McKinney well either. She and Mom didn't get along. Mom called her stingy when she was being nice, worse things when she wasn't.

I regret not knowing my grandmother better. Now that I'm old enough to have learned some hard truths about my mom, I think maybe we would have gotten along and it would have been nicer to have a relationship beyond the occasional phone call and a birthday card in the mail stuffed with cash my brother could steal.

We're meeting at Kinnara, Tuan's Vietnamese restaurant. It's the nicest place in Here, and the food's great. Also, dogs are allowed on the patio, so I've got Princess with me.

I arrive first. Uncle Robert's driving in from Buffalo to meet with me, and he said he's running a few minutes late. That's a long drive to make when we probably could have just talked over the phone, but whatever.

"Hey man." Tuan claps me on the back, bringing a

bowl of water over for Princess. "How're things at On the Rocks?"

We shoot the shit for a bit. We use a lot of the same suppliers, and while I don't order the food for the bar, Tuan and I have always exchanged notes. He and Hunter are close, too.

Suddenly, he gives me a funny look, glancing at something over my shoulder and then back at me. "That's not your dad, is it?"

Tuan knows I don't know who my dad is, but I turn around and understand the question. My uncle's here, and since I take after my mom, I'm not surprised he can see the resemblance. I wave him over. "My uncle."

Uncle Robert arrives at the table and I stand. He offers me a firm handshake, and I introduce him to Tuan, who excuses himself, giving Princess one last head pat.

"Who's this?" Robert bends down to greet my dog. He's dressed in slacks and a polo: your typical dad look. He does look like me. Full head of sandy dark hair, the same nose shape my mom and I used to have—me before I broke it in a fight in high school, my mom's before . . . well . . .

"Princess," I say. "Careful, she's a—"

Princess sticks her nose in my uncle's crotch and he lets out a high-pitched "oof."

"—crotch sniffer."

"Not used to that," he says. "My dog only comes up to my knee on her hind legs."

"A little one," I remark, and we take our seats.

"What's good here?"

I throw out a couple suggestions, Tuan comes back to take our order, and the two of us sit back in our chairs.

"Do you see your mom much, Morgan?"

"She calls me every once in a while," I say carefully.

"She lives near here, right?"

I nod and point away from the ski lodge. "Just outside of town."

"How's she doing?"

Well, she's usually hanging out with bad people, when she calls she asks me for money, and she fucking enables my brother. I shrug. "You'll have to ask her."

Uncle Robert grunts. "Fair enough. How about you? You work at the ski lodge, right?"

I tell him about my job, and he asks a few questions. I remembered correctly; he's an accountant. Not a lot of common ground.

"You're a skier, then?"

"Oh yeah," I say. "Grew up on that mountain. Used to bus us over right after school."

Our food comes, and Uncle Robert tells me about skiing out west, places like Steamboat Springs and Whistler. He's dismissive of skiing here, which, like, fine, we're not deep snow and powder, but it's beautiful in its own way. And when you grow up out here, you're used to it. If we traded places, we'd both probably be out on our asses—I've never skied in powder before, but no one complains about that. Put a Colorado skier on our slopes and they become whiny little babies about the ice.

It's a nice chat, but I can't help but wonder why we're here.

Our plates get cleared, and I decide enough bullshitting. "Uncle Robert, why are you here? Not that I'm not enjoying our chat, but . . ."

He grins. "You're wondering why the hell I drove all the way here just to take you out to lunch?"

"Well . . . yeah."

Uncle Robert leans forward, folding his hands together.

"As I'm sure you know, I'm not close with your mom. She's . . . complicated."

I nod. That's putting it mildly.

"She and your grandmother barely talked. That wasn't your grandma's choice, but that's the way it played out. So I wanted to talk to you personally and give you a heads-up."

I brace myself.

"The bad news is that your grandmother passed away with a fairly comfortable portfolio."

What a rich-person thing to say. *Portfolio.* Also, that doesn't sound like bad news, but I wait for the other shoe to drop.

"Your mother and I inherit the money fifty-fifty, but there are stipulations. I'm both the executor of Ada's estate and the trustee of the trusts."

I stare at him.

"I'm responsible for stewarding the money your mother inherits and making sure she follows the requirements of the will. She's not going to be happy about that."

I have a guess on what the will stipulates, and saying Mom won't be happy is probably an understatement. "What happens if Mom doesn't follow the rules?"

"If five years pass, the trust falls equally to you and your brother, with the same stipulations."

"Okay. So . . ."

"Unless your mother and brother significantly clean up their act, you stand to inherit a good bit of money in five years, and then double it in ten."

That stuns me. I knew Grandma was richer than we were, but a "good bit of money" coming from Uncle Robert sounds like maybe a lot?

"A word of advice, son?" he continues.

"Yeah, sure." I gesture for him to go on.

"Don't count on the money."

My face falls.

"Not because I don't think you're going to get it," he adds. "Although . . ." He shrugs. "You never know. People have gotten clean for a lot worse reasons. But I'm just saying, the general advice is that you don't plan your finances around having an inheritance. It's a good way to ensure that if you don't get it, you're screwed, and if you do get it, you've already earmarked it for too much and it gets away from you. Have you read any financial literacy books?"

I shake my head. I just chuck money into a savings account.

"I'll send you some of my favorites." He claps a hand on my shoulder. "I have faith that you're a smart man and you'll learn."

I don't know what gave him that idea. I am my mother's son after all.

"There's one more thing."

More? I've just learned that I might have an inheritance from my grandmother. That's a lot to process, even if it's down the road and maybe . . . if Mom has to stay clean, I think it's ninety-five percent likely to happen. Those odds are pretty fucking good.

Too bad it's not coming in time to chip in to buy the lodge.

Uncle Robert reaches into his pocket. "Your grandmother had a codicil. Do you know what that is?"

"No, sir."

He pulls out a small box. It's blue and velvet, like a jewelry box. "It's a handwritten addition to the will that your grandmother wrote, laying out what personal effects go where. It's easier to execute than a will. Estates take a while to close when they're as complicated as your grandmother's, and I have a feeling I'll be hearing from your mom and things will get nasty pretty quickly. But, I'm able to give you this, which your grandmother left directly for you."

He sets the box on the table. I glance up at him, bewildered, and he nods at it. "Go ahead."

I pick it up. It is a jewelry box, and it's heavier than I expected. I flip open the lid and . . .

There's the biggest fucking diamond ring I've ever seen in my life. Not that I've seen many diamonds in person. But this one's huge; no wonder the box is so heavy. It's even bigger than Mrs. Gardiner's, who still wears the ring her late husband gave her.

It's a rectangular shape, surrounded by light blue stones. I try to think of what stone is light blue, but I have no idea. Sapphires are dark, right? And the diamond is the size of a disco ball for ants. Seriously, the sun catches the light and it sparkles and glitters on the tablecloth like a tiny party in . . .

Wait a minute.

I sit up straight. "My grandmother left this for me?"

"Yup," Uncle Robert says, a faint smile on his face.

I snap the box closed and put it back on the table between us, like if I can't see it, I can't lose it or break it or otherwise damage this family heirloom. "Why?"

"Well, you are her oldest grandchild, and I think she feels . . . felt. I think she felt guilty about not knowing you better."

An uncomfortable feeling sits in my chest. Money makes people weird. She couldn't spend time with me in real life, so now I get this ring instead? That's ridiculous.

Uncle Robert reaches into his pocket again and I eye him warily. Is there more? Matching earrings? A fancy watch? What the fuck?

Instead, it's an envelope.

"The ring was appraised a few years ago, the last time Mom updated her will. If you're going to keep it, you should insure it, and they may take this appraisal or they may ask for a new one."

I open the envelope, which is unsealed, and pull the stack of papers out. I scan the official-looking letter until I arrive at the number at the bottom.

"Holy shit." I jump to my feet, my chair hitting the ground behind me and my hips knocking into the table. It's enough to tip a full glass of water over, which spills through the mesh table and onto Princess. I lunge for the glass but accidentally send the ring box flying.

Princess is barking, and Uncle Robert, brushing water off his lap, laughs.

Tuan comes out to help us clean up and by the time Princess is settled and somewhat dry, I finally think about the ring.

I look around and spot it at one of the tables nearby in the hands of another patron. The box is open and three sets of eyes ping-pong back and forth between me and the ring.

"Janet. Willow. Mrs. Gardiner." I nod at all three of the older women. Just my luck that they're here today.

Miss Mullins and Miss Bright (Janet and Willow, respectively) insist I use their first names, but they've been Miss Mullins and Miss Bright since I was a boy, so it's hard to think of them as Janet and Willow. (Mrs. Gardiner has never told me to use her first name.) Miss Mullins is the one holding the ring box, and she snaps it closed. "Morgan Law. I didn't know you were dating someone." She peers at me with curiosity. Today she's wearing a shirt that has Ruth Bader Ginsburg on the front and says, "Fight for the things you care about."

"Who?" Miss Bright asks, her braids over one shoulder and her movements languid. Not even a giant diamond ring can faze the chillest woman I've known in my life.

"Is it Melissa?" Miss Mullins asks, making me do a double take. Melissa and I had a discreet hookup a few months ago while she was broken up with her on-again-off-again boyfriend. How the hell does Miss Mullins even know about it? "She's such a nice girl."

"Good grief, Janet. She's back together with Charles," Mrs. Gardiner snaps. "A nice girl shouldn't have taste that bad."

Kind of mean, but also true. Charles is a walking red flag.

"Women date according to their self-esteem," Miss Mullins says sadly. "Think about that."

"It's not Melissa," I say, and put my palm out for the ring box.

Miss Mullins reluctantly places it in my hand and I deflect their attempts at further conversation and turn back to Uncle Robert. Once I get settled back into the seat, I look at the appraisal again, just to make sure I didn't misread it or imagine the number.

Nope. Still huge. Still five figures. Still a fucking engagement ring.

"Holy shit," I say again. "This is enough to buy . . ."

It's more than my car's worth. It's more than I was trying to save up for a down payment on my own bar. *It's more than Hunter was asking me for on Monday.*

Holy shit. We *could* buy the lodge.

Mining
Dog Shit

MORGAN

"THERE YOU ARE." BAILEY'S VOICE COMES FROM THE house, where I've left the back door open. Princess, who was snoozing underneath my chair, startles awake and lurches to her feet. She ping-pongs off three of the four chair legs before she zeroes in on Bailey. If Princess were a Great Dane, I probably would have ridden her up the stairs of the porch.

Bailey opens the screen door before Princess busts through it and they greet each other with enthusiasm.

It's chilly today, and Princess and I must have been out here for a few hours, since Bailey said she'd be here at three. We alternated between napping (Princess) and reading (me) and playing fetch or tug-of-war.

True to his word, Uncle Robert didn't just send me a list of books to read, he sent me the e-books as gifts. He said he got help from one of his daughters to figure out how to do it, and then I had to figure out how to accept the gift and get it open on my phone.

So I'm spending my Friday before work reading a book that claims it'll teach me how to be rich by some guy that's got a Netflix show.

I turn the screen off and put the phone in my pocket, following Princess to greet Bailey. "Hey, thanks for coming by."

"Of course." Bailey's bent down, Princess leaning against her legs, nearly knocking her over. She's wearing her hair up, a full face of makeup, and a crisp button-down shirt.

And beneath that are sweatpants and sneakers.

"You didn't have to dress up for me," I tease.

"Ha," she says. "I had a meeting right before this. On Zoom."

"Ah," I say, and lead her inside. Something smells good. "Did you bring food?"

Princess runs headlong into the house, running a circuit around the first floor. You'd think I didn't just spend all day wearing her out.

"Yeah. Silas made lasagna last night and I haven't had lunch. I brought enough to share."

"Have I told you you're my favorite best friend's girlfriend ever?"

She rolls her eyes and tells me I'm her favorite bartender, and we tease each other while we heat up lunch.

Bailey was a shy kid, and Hunter was overprotective. She struggled to fit in when we were growing up, mostly on account of some assholes bullying her for her size.

"What's Silas up to today?" I invited him to come too, but he was busy.

"House showings," she says as we settle at my little kitchen table. "Is this a Rory weekend?"

"Hell yeah it is."

"Still don't know why she comes to town?"

I shake my head. "No clue. It makes me wonder if someday she'll just never come back. I'll only have fond memories of her scowl to keep me warm at night."

Bailey rolls her eyes. "Along with any of the town's single women."

"I'll be too heartbroken," I tell her, putting a hand over my chest and trying to affect an air of a broken heart.

She squints at me. "Are you trying to swoon? Or is the lasagna getting to you?"

"Shut up. The lasagna's great."

"Yeah." Bailey smiles down at her plate. "He can cook and clean and . . . do other stuff." She darts a cheeky glance up at me and I laugh.

"He's the whole package. Good job."

"Thanks."

I clear my throat. "So . . . I could use some advice."

Bailey perks up. "Sure. What's up?"

"Do you remember how a few years ago your mom gave Hunter your grandmother's engagement ring?"

Bailey looks at me curiously. "Yes. I'm surprised you remember that."

It was memorable because Hunter was really pissed at his mom for giving him the ring. Well, not for giving him the ring so much as saying something about Bailey not ever going to need it. We get an earful from Hunter about how little their mother thinks of Bailey, even though she's a gorgeous, voluptuous woman (who I think of like a sister).

Bailey's mom sucks.

Something in Bailey's face shifts. "Wait a minute . . .

Hunter's not . . . he's not giving the ring to Silas, right?" Her voice has taken on a panicked edge.

"No, no, no," I assure her.

"Oh good," she says, blowing out a big breath. At my raised eyebrows, she quickly clarifies. "I mean, not *good*, like, I don't want to marry Silas. I mean . . . it's only been two months since I moved here."

"Right." I suppress a smile.

"Obviously I want to marry Silas someday." I laugh, and she puts her face in her hands and takes a deep breath before chuckling at herself. "Have you seen the ring? Hunter offered it to me, even suggested I make the diamond into a necklace, but to be honest with you it's kind of hideous. But anyway, why are you bringing this up?"

I explain about how my uncle gave me the ring from Grandma. "I know you and Hunter took it to someone in the city, so maybe you'd know of a jeweler to talk to or . . . like . . . I don't even know what I need to do. Uncle Robert said stuff about an appraisal and insurance."

"So the rumors are true, huh?"

I cover my face with my hands and groan. "Ugh, yes." Since meeting with my uncle I've ignored no fewer than twenty text messages asking about me getting engaged. I've also had plenty of people at On the Rocks ask about it, and, inexplicably, two past hookups came out of the woodwork and hit me up for booty calls.

I declined them both.

Obviously the rumors came from the gossipy older ladies. Miss Mullins didn't even look chagrined when I confronted her about it.

"Can I see the ring?"

"Sure." I stand and retrieve the stepladder from beside

the fridge. Using it, I reach up to the top of the cabinets above my sink and feel around for the box.

Bailey smothers a laugh. "You're keeping it up there?"

"I'm worried Princess might eat it! She's too curious about anything that's nose height or lower. Remember that time she ate Kit's sock? Or the Monopoly piece? Or the key to the bar's lockbox?" I could go on. I locate the box and step down from the ladder. "The last thing I need is to go mining dog shit to find the most valuable thing I own. Or worse: take her to the vet for expensive surgery. Wouldn't that be ironic."

I pop open the box and Bailey gasps.

"Holy fuck. This is gorgeous."

"I know, right? Gorgeous and only mildly terrifying."

"Terrifying because . . . ?"

"When I sell it," I explain, "this will be the most money I've ever had in my life. I don't want to fuck it up."

Bailey hums in understanding. "Can I try it on?"

"Sure. Just don't get it stuck."

She slides the ring up her right ring finger but it's too big. She slips it on the middle one and it's perfect.

"I wanted to ask you about that too."

Bailey is too busy staring at the ring and twisting her hand back and forth. Then she blinks up at me. "Sorry, what?"

I shift uncomfortably in my seat. I've never talked to any of my friends about money, and it was always such a sore subject in my house. "When I sell the ring, that would give me enough money to help buy the lodge. And I know, you and Silas have already said you are in, so you're not entirely unbiased here. But you're also—I think—one of the most financially smart people I know."

Bailey puts her hand down. "How do you figure that?"

I tick my fingers off. "Good job in the city plus being

able to buy into the lodge. You probably have a 401(k). The rest of us are hot messes."

She frowns. "You're not a hot mess. You live in a small town. Things are different here."

"Exactly my point. So . . . what do you think I should do? Should I buy into the lodge? Or is that a dumb idea?"

Bailey frowns and then pelts me with a ton of questions. Some of them I have rough answers to—how much I've saved up, what the estimated costs are of opening my own bar—and some of them make me feel really dumb—no, I don't have a retirement account and yes, I do have credit card debt. I have to pull out my laptop and we hunch over looking at numbers together.

What really gets us is that if I buy my own bar, I'm starting from scratch. I'd be competing with whoever bought the lodge (if they keep it running) and outside of Herevians, I'd have to build up my new bar's reputation. I'd have to get a new liquor permit, too, and a whole slew of other stuff that's tabled to worry about until I have the money.

Which is now, I guess.

"So." Bailey finally leans back and crosses her arms. "To be honest, the smart thing would be to invest the money."

My heart sinks, and Bailey points at me.

"That's what I really wanted to know. That's disappointing to you, and that probably tells us more than the numbers do." She pivots in her chair, facing me head-on. "Moving out to Here wasn't a smart financial decision for me. I worked really hard over the years to get raises and promotions, to always be at the table, and to take every extra assignment I could. I *know* that I'm leaving money behind by living here and working remotely. When the Zoom meetings end, all the people in the room keep talking and I'm left out of that conversation. Even more so than I already was as a woman in a man's field."

"Right. Loving Silas wasn't a head move, it was a heart move."

"Exactly. So if you're going to sell the ring instead of keep it, even if it doesn't make financial sense, you'll want your own bar. And the lodge might be the best way to do that." She grins slyly. "As long as you're willing to have Hunter, me, and Silas as business partners."

I should focus on the business partners part. But instead my brain snags on the first thing she says. "Keep the ring?"

Bailey slides it off her finger and holds it out to me. "Yeah. It's beautiful and a family heirloom. Someday when you propose you might wish you'd kept it."

I pinch the band of the ring between my fingers and stare down at it. I've never thought about proposing to anyone before, but it hits me that I have in my hands the possibility of one of the best pranks I've ever pulled.

God, Rory's going to laugh her ass off at me.

He Smote Me
Long Ago

Rory

It's been a hell of a fucking day. No—two days. I've been here since Saturday morning when I got the call that Grandma wasn't feeling well.

The community Grandma lives in has medical facilities in addition to the assisted living, hospice area, and independent living, where Grandma lives.

For now.

She's got a fever. The doctors have run a few tests and they think it's viral, which means there's not much to do other than treat the symptoms and let her body take care of it.

I'm sitting in one of the chairs next to Grandma's hospital bed, reading, while she sleeps. It's five forty in the evening. On a Sunday. If this was a regular Sunday visit, I'd be speeding toward Morgan's bar right now.

On the bed, Grandma shifts and her eyes blink open. "Deborah?" Her voice is muffled through the mask.

Deborah's my mom, Grandma's daughter. She's mistaken me for her twice since she's been sick, and the doctor says that happens. It scares the shit out of me though—Grandma with a sharp mind is a force of nature. Grandma with dementia or Alzheimer's would be a nightmare.

"It's me, Grandma." I lean in closer so she can see me. I'm wearing a mask, too, just in case, so I make sure she can see my eyes. "Rory."

"Rory?" There's a pause, and then her voice gets more confident. "Rory."

"Are you feeling any better?"

"I'm not dying yet." The snap is weak, but it's there. I bite back a smile. Attitude is good.

This morning when Grandma woke up confused, it lingered longer and she cried. It scared the shit out of me. "We only have each other. I don't want to leave you," she'd said between tears.

Once I'd gotten her back to sleep, I'd cried too. My eyes are still puffy and it doesn't help that I hear her voice telling me she doesn't want to leave me every time I close them.

Grandma closes her eyes again. "What time is it?"

I check my watch, even though I don't need to. "Five forty-five."

"You should go," she mumbles. "I can feel your boredom even when I'm asleep."

God, the snark of this woman. I'm not that bad, am I?

"I'm fine."

She cracks an eye open. "Alone is what you are. Don't you have some handsome bartender to go visit?"

"It's fine, Grandma."

"I'm not going to die in the next few hours. Go take a break," she insists.

"I'm fine." I can out-stubborn her any day.

Grandma's eyes snap open and she grabs the handles of the bed, trying to push herself up to sitting.

I jump to my feet and hover. "Grandma! Stop."

"I will not." She's sitting up but she's wheezing, and the beeps on the heart rate monitor are getting faster. "You're going to go to that bar and by god you are going to flirt with that bartender until he asks you out for the umpteenth time and you're going to say yes tonight or so help me god, I will die on you!"

"Grandma," I scold, appalled. "You shouldn't talk like that."

"What, threaten you with my death? Buckle up, missy. I'm driving this bus."

"I know you believe in God," I huff. "And I know he's going to smite you after that speech."

"He smote me . . . long ago." Grandma breathes hard for a few moments. "Now are you . . . going or not?"

"Arghhhh!" I run a hand through my hair, which is loose around my shoulders since I washed it last night and haven't ridden my bike today. "You are infuriating." I point a finger at her. "Fine. I'm going."

"Ha," she says, and then collapses back into the bed.

"If you die while I'm gone, I'm cremating you," I threaten. "And the service will be in the gymnasium instead of the chapel. I'll tell them that was your last wish."

"Eh," she says. Her heart rate is getting back to normal and her breathing is easier. "No one's coming to my service anyway."

It takes me some time to get her settled back down and I procrastinate until I'm pretty sure Grandma fakes being asleep.

I step out into the hallway and one of the nurses at the station looks up and smiles.

"How's she doing?"

"Bitchy."

She laughs. "Is she sleeping?"

"Faking it, probably." I sigh and walk toward the door. A few paces away, I stop.

And sigh again.

Grandma says she's not going to die, and as much as I'd like to think she's made a deal with the devil, she's just a woman. An old woman, who's so scared of dying alone, she's pushing me to find someone so the same thing doesn't happen to me.

I turn around. The nurse glances up and shakes a finger at me. "Go," she says. "We'll take good care of her and you need a break. I know there's no one else to call, but you've got to take care of yourself first. She'll be happy to see you tomorrow and we'll call if there are any changes."

Even I don't backtalk a nurse, so I turn around and make my way outside. I'm going to be later than usual, and even though we don't have anything as formal as a date, Morgan will probably worry about me. I strap my helmet on, ignoring my loose hair, and fire my bike up.

I ease out onto the street and head toward Here. Grandma's living community is another thirty or so miles northwest, away from the city. It's for rich New Yorkers—like my grandmother—who want to spend their retirement enjoying the scenic beauty and small-town charm of the Catskills.

It's all small country roads, and it'll be a dream to ride my bike through in the fall. Right now though, it's late August and summer was having its last gasp today. The wind whipping past feels good, but my leather jacket is too hot when I stop at lights and signs. My favorites sights are the bright yellow ones, trees that change suddenly, like someone's come through and sucked all the blue out by the roots and changed the green to yellow.

In thirty-five minutes, I'm at the bar. The cowbell clangs overhead and this time I pause to look around. Everything's back to normal, the somber mood from two weeks ago gone. The music's loud and upbeat, the old ladies are in the corner booth, and I spot a few buckets of beers on the tables.

And then my eyes meet Morgan's. His smile goes nuclear and my shoulders drop in relief. No more kicked-puppy look. We're back to happy-go-lucky Morgan and all feels right in the world again.

By the time I sit down he's got a bottle of my favorite beer waiting. I take a big swig, finishing nearly half the bottle before I set it down.

"How are you today, my queen?"

"Better now," I answer.

His eyes twinkle, and he walks down the bar, probably to put my order in. I take another sip, and then the music gets turned down.

"Excuse me, everyone!" Morgan shouts. He holds his hands up. "Excuse me!"

The din slowly fades and all the faces in the bar turn toward him. He starts walking back toward me, a massive smile on his face. What is he up to?

"Everyone, thank you for your attention. I've got something I want to say here to Rory."

Uh-oh. He's standing in front of me now, and the bar is dead quiet. Nerves flutter in my stomach. Grandma's words are loud in my head.

. . . you're going to say yes tonight or so help me god, I will die on you!

Oh my god. I'm finally going to say yes.

"Rory . . ." he announces. Then his brows draw together and his voice returns to a normal level. "Rory . . . uhh . . . what's your last name?"

"Morgan, what are you doing?" I hiss.

"What's your last name?" he whispers.

"Fox. Why—"

"Rory Fox!" He's back to speaking loudly again. Morgan reaches into his pocket and pulls something out. It catches the light, flashing as he holds it between two fingers and offers it to me. I have a split second to realize it's a diamond ring before he blows my mind. "Rory Fox, will you marry me?"

Freshly Fucked

MORGAN

RORY'S EYES ARE THE SIZE OF DINNER PLATES AS SHE STARES down at my grandmother's ring. The whole bar is deathly quiet, waiting on her answer.

Any moment now, she's going to react. Worst-case scenario, she rolls her eyes and looks unimpressed. Best-case scenario, she laughs her ass off, tells me I'm an idiot, and I say something smooth and clever, like "Well, if you don't want to marry me, then how about a first date?"

I may have thought about this too much.

Finally, Rory looks up. Her mouth hangs open, and yeah, I know that feeling. The ring is shocking as hell. She probably thinks it's fake though. Who would believe a small-town bartender like me has a giant diamond ring just lying around to use as a prank?

She stares at me for a beat. And then she says the last goddamn thing I expect to hear.

"Yes."

Noise erupts all around us and I stare back at her. She said yes?

She said yes!

I throw back my head and laugh.

"No, wait!" she says, eyes widening even farther, but it's too late. No one but me can hear her over the noise of cheering and congratulating. She reaches out and grabs my collar, pulling me toward her. "What the fuck, Morgan?" She has to shout over the noise.

"You said yes!" I shout back. "No take backs!"

"That's not how this works!"

She starts dragging me down the bar by my flannel, her long strides and narrowed eyes making everyone move out of her way. They were up on their feet anyway.

When she gets to the pass-through, she steps behind the bar and pushes me toward the storage room. Over her shoulder, I see Hunter slip past the crowd at the bar and give me a chin lift, letting me know he'll take care of things out here.

My shoulders hit the door. Rory flings it open and we both go stumbling in. It bounces off the wall and closes behind her, muffling the noise of the bar and cutting off all the light.

"Fuck," she says in the dark. "Where's the light switch?"

"It's over—" I reach for the wall toward the door and bump into Rory reaching in the opposite direction. Our arms tangle, and I hit something soft.

"Ouch!"

"Sorry."

"That was my boob!" Her voice is full of indignation.

I try again, dodge a flailing arm, and we take steps toward each other.

Instinctively, I reach out to steady us both, and the ring, which I somehow managed to hold on to all the way around the bar, flies out of my hand and clinks on something.

I've got my hand on Rory, though, and any other thoughts fly out my head, including the light switch. My hand settles on her waist, just above the band of her jeans and somehow tucked under her leather jacket to that sliver of skin that shows when she puts her helmet on or takes it off.

I may have watched her from the window a few times.

Rory slaps around until she finds the switch and we're lit up in the fluorescent glow of the storage room.

"What. The. Hell." She punctuates each word with a light back-handed smack on my chest and shoulders.

I grab one of her wrists and hold it above our heads. She smacks me with the other one, but it's got less oomph to it. "Me? What about you? You said yes!"

"And I clearly didn't mean it!" She's given up on smacking me but I keep ahold of her wrist.

"How was I supposed to know that? Or anyone else in the bar either?"

"Why on earth did you do that?"

"Because I thought it would be funny."

Now I get the eye roll I was expecting. I let go of her hand.

"Help me find the ring. I dropped it in here somewhere."

We fall to our hands and knees (after Rory huffs in exasperation) and start looking. The storeroom is full of standing shelves with dry bar supplies. The ring can't have gone far, but it's dark beneath the shelves and also a bit grimy so Rory pulls out her phone and turns on the flashlight.

After a few minutes looking for the ring, I start to get nervous. What if we never find it? Jesus, no wonder Uncle Robert told me not to count on the money until I actually had it. I'm sweating thinking about the windfall I might have lost in the deep dark corners of this place.

Rory sits back on her heels. "What does it look like?"

My face is pressed against the floor, my fingers running along the far wall. If either of us were in our right mind, I'd probably tease her about staring at my ass, which is pointed right at her while I'm hunched over. "You just spent like five minutes gaping at it, you don't know what it looks like?"

"I was stunned speechless by the sheer audacity of your confidence."

"How about if you find any ring, you run it by me and I'll tell you if it's the right one."

"Smart-ass," she mutters. Two seconds later: "Found it."

I yank my hand back from underneath the shelves and tell myself I'll talk Hunter into hiring Kit to come in and do a deep clean back here. "Thank god. Where is it?" I've got a bar rag in my back pocket, so I take it out and wipe the cobwebs off my hands.

I shift around so I'm facing her and she points. There's a mug on one of the shelves that we use to store Sharpies and pens to label boxes and fill out inventory, and the ring is caught on one of the pens, the diamond sitting on the lip of the mug like a cheeky little fucker.

"Jesus Christ. If that had fallen into the mug we never would have found it."

"That's concerning," Rory remarks.

She stands and leaves it to me to pluck the ring out.

"Okay," I say, staring at the ring. "We know why I asked you. But I still don't know why you said yes."

"I'm not going to marry you."

I shrug. The lady doth protest too much. "Maybe."

"What do you mean maybe?" She's getting worked up again.

"Maybe it was a Freudian slip?" I raise both hands in a what-are-you-gonna-do gesture. "And you still haven't answered the question."

Rory looks away, crossing her arms and biting her lip.

I wait.

"My grandma's sick, okay?" she tells the floor.

My face falls. "Oh, shit. Is she gonna be all right?"

"Maybe. Probably. She's normally in pretty good health for her age and I think this is just an infection." She kicks one of the shelves gently with the toe of her boot. "It's just the two of us, and she's always ragging on me to find someone. She doesn't want me—she doesn't want to die alone."

Rory finally looks up at me. "I'm sorry, all right? It was just a weak moment. It would make Grandma happy and I wasn't thinking clearly."

I look down at the ring in my hand. I'm not alone in life—I have my friends, and every day I get to see familiar faces.

Herevians that love me and care about me.

I don't know what Rory does for a job, or where she lives, or who her friends are. But if she's that desperate . . .

This time, I do it properly. I get down on one knee. Rory glares at me. "Rory Fox, will you marry me?"

"Shut up."

"I'm serious," I protest. "Well, kind of. Look, if this is something that would make you happy, let's do it. Let's pretend a little. Let's tell your grandma we're engaged, and let her enjoy it for a while."

"She's not dying. I hope. I mean . . . she's sick right now, but the doctors are optimistic and she's too ornery to go down without a fight."

"So we pretend for a while and then call it off. Say it didn't work out."

Rory rolls her eyes. She turns and walks away, as far as she can in this little room, and then turns back. "We barely know each other. No one's going to believe we're engaged."

Okay, my knee is starting to ache. I rise and gesture toward the outside world. "Everyone out there knows you've got me hook, line, and sinker. And they just watched you accept my proposal. Hell yeah, they're going to believe it. They'll think I finally wore you down."

She lets out a weak laugh. "So what, I'll wear the ring? You'll come meet my grandma? Then what?"

I stretch my arms out. "Ball's in your court, my queen."

Silence falls between us. I lift the ring.

Her arms drop to her sides. "Fine, okay."

"That's exactly the words I've always wanted to hear when I proposed to the woman of my dreams," I tease. "Give me your hand."

Rory holds out her left hand and turns her head away, but I see her watching out of the corner of her eye.

I slide my fingers on her hand, the tips trailing over her palm. Her nails are short and rounded, trim and pretty. I line the ring up to her finger and take a deep breath.

A moment of doubt creeps in. What am I doing? Rory just said that we barely know each other and I'm about to trust her with an expensive family heirloom. She could sell it or lose it or . . .

Fuck. *I* can't sell the ring as long as we're pretending to be engaged. Shit, shit, shit.

I look up at Rory and she's facing me now, watching me, her eyes dark and serious.

I slide the ring on.

It fits perfectly, and we both let out a breath.

I pull my hands away and wipe the perspiration off on my jeans. Who knew a fake engagement could make me break out into a sweat like this?

Rory stares at the ring. "I guess we have to go back out there?"

"Yeah. Oh, but hang on."

I start to unbutton my shirt.

"What are you doing?" she hisses.

"Hang *on.*" I get about halfway down and then rebutton, purposefully missing a hole. I run my hands through my hair, grabbing fistfuls of it and tugging. Then I peer at Rory.

"Your hair is already pretty wild. How about I just take some of this—"

I lean forward and tilt her chin up. Carefully, I swipe my thumb over her lips, smearing the edge. It's only about halfway through that I realize how much I've invaded her personal space. Our toes are almost touching, and I'm standing close enough that I can make out the dark brown ring around her blown-out pupils.

She presses her lips firmly together and glances away.

Right.

I take my thumb and swipe it over my own lips, attempting to smear some lipstick around. She may not be ready for me to kiss her, but at least we'll *look* freshly fucked.

Rory's watching me again.

I reach down and grab her left hand in my right,

twining our fingers together. "You ready for this?" I ask, one hand on the doorknob.

"You're a menace."

"You love it." I fling the door open, and we step out into the bar as a newly engaged couple to the sound of catcalls and cheers.

A Soft Spot

Morgan

I've got Rory's number.

Literally and figuratively, and it's adorable.

We swapped digits so we could plan the Big Reveal to her grandma and it's obvious that her grandma is a soft spot for her.

In a weird way.

Rory texts me the address where we're going to meet and follows it up with a bunch of rapid-fire warnings.

My Queen

Meet me at noon at the Buckingham.

It's the fancy restaurant in the building. The front desk will tell you where to go.

> You know what? I'll just meet you out front.

> At 11:55

> Can you dress up?

> Do you own a tie?

> If you flirt with my grandmother I swear to god I will stab you with one of the fancy forks I never know when to use.

> GRANDMA WILL INSULT YOU. DO NOT ENGAGE.

> I mean it, Morgan.

Texts like that come through all the way up until I leave for lunch on Sunday. Hunter's watching the bar for me, and I told him I'd be back in the afternoon before happy hour starts. It's been two weeks since my proposal to Rory, and it's been the talk of the town.

I drive my truck up to the main building of the community. It's a whole damn complex out here—there are signs directing cars to places like *Honor Garden* and *The Dr. and Mrs. Goldstein Active Gymnasium*. It's half apartment complex, half university campus. I never knew a hideaway like this existed out here.

Before I even park I spot Rory at the front door at the drop-off carport. Her arms are crossed and she's scowling at me—or maybe she's just scowling at the wind playing with her loose hair.

I pick a spot and hop out, jogging to greet her.

"Hey."

She looks me up and down. I'm wearing blue slacks, a white button-down, and a festive, ski-themed tie. It's not Christmassy, it's just bright. The blue of the scarves the skiers are wearing matches my pants.

Rory rolls her eyes, pressing her lips to hold in a smile.

I chose not to point out my matching socks to her. I'll save those for later as an emergency eye-roll contingency plan.

"You look great," I tell her. She's wearing wide-legged slacks and a blouse, both black. Her hair is neither in braids nor a windblown mess like every other time I've seen her. Instead, it's smoothed down, the waves falling over her shoulder, though the breeze is toying with it. Her finger's bare, though. "Where's the ring?"

She pats her pocket. "I've been with Grandma all day. I thought it would be better if we tell her together."

Aw, she needed her emotional support fake fiancé with her.

"You got it. I'll follow your lead today."

She nods and turns on her heel, leading me in. I have to check in at the front desk for security and then we go down a winding set of turns until we're in a literal ballroom. It sounds like something out of *Bridgerton*, too: clinking glasses, a low hum of conversation, and even a string quartet piped in.

Rory waves to the hostess and beelines for a four-top table with a little old white lady sitting alone, her chair angled out so she can see the door. She spots us and rises to her feet, grabbing a cane to help her.

Rory's grandma's gaze is hawkish. She scrutinizes me, and then her gaze falls on her granddaughter again and I realize maybe we should have held hands or I should have put my palm on the small of Rory's back. Something couple-like.

"So," she says as we approach. "You're Morgan the bartender."

"Yes, ma'am." I offer her a hand. "Nice to meet you, Mrs. . . ."

I flounder. I don't know if this is Rory's paternal grandmother or maternal grandmother.

"Mrs. Patterson," she sniffs. "I guess your persistence has paid off, young man."

I grin at her. "Yes, ma'am."

"You must be the pushy sort."

"When I need to be."

She harrumphs at that.

"Grandma," Rory says. "Sit down so we can sit too."

"Fine, fine." Mrs. Patterson waves her cane in the air, but moves to take her seat. A server appears to push her chair in.

Before that server can move to Rory's side, I grab the chair for her and pull it out. "My queen."

Mrs. Patterson snorts. It sounds a lot like Rory's snorts.

Once we are seated, I look over the menu with running commentary from Mrs. Patterson, who's got an opinion about everything, and Rory protesting every other word.

I put the menu down about halfway through the diatribe, and when she's done, I lean forward. "Rory told me you were sick last week. How are you feeling now?"

"Fine, except a nurse still comes to take my vitals every day. And you just know I'm going to get a bill charging me for all that."

She rants for a while about the medical bills and then asks me, "When did you two meet?"

The conversational change catches me by surprise and I jump to answer. "At my bar. I guess it was . . . three months ago, right?"

Rory nods.

Mrs. Patterson's sharp eyes assess me. "And what drew you to my Rory?"

It feels like a test. I look over at Rory, whose eyes are

wide with panic. I grin at her. "The first time I saw her smile. I'd just called her my queen and she tried to hide it. But I saw."

"She's not good at taking compliments."

Rory throws her hands up. "How would you know? You never compliment me."

Mrs. Patterson gasps. "I compliment you all the time."

They bicker for a bit, Mrs. Patterson giving examples and Rory telling her they aren't compliments, they're observations, until Rory switches topics.

"Grandma, wasn't that the new couple you were making friends with?" She gestures to a (relatively) young pair that's being led through the tables in our direction. They look to be in their early seventies.

Mrs. Patterson glares at them. "Criminals!" she announces. "They should be ashamed of themselves."

Rory's jaw drops. "What are you talking about?"

"I mean this place is turning into a white-collar jailhouse. Who's going to move in next? Bernie Madoff?"

"I think he's dead," I say.

"What do you mean criminal?" Rory asks again.

"He worked for Wells Fargo," Mrs. Patterson snaps. "All those predatory loans. How they're still in business I'll never understand."

"Grandma, I doubt he was actually the one giving out loans."

"He was management. Even worse!"

Rory puts her face in her hands. "Okay, we're getting off topic."

"We have a topic?"

"Grandma, there's something I—"

A server interrupts Rory. "Are you ready to order?"

We are. We do. It's a process, because Mrs. Patterson

asks a lot of questions and Rory tells her to be nicer to the staff.

Watching Rory and her grandmother is like watching a tennis match. I sip my water, reveling in this reveal of Rory's life.

Mrs. Patterson turns back to her granddaughter as soon as the server walks away. Her eyebrows bunch together. "You look pale. You're not knocked up, are you?"

I choke on my water.

Mrs. Patterson peers at me. "I hope you're better in bed than you are at drinking."

"Grandma." Rory closes her eyes like she's praying. "Morgan and I have something to tell you." She leans back, digs the ring out of her pocket, and shoves it on her finger. "We're getting married. I know it's fast, but you got engaged to Grandpa after two weeks of dating, so, you know . . ."

Rory trails off.

Two cosmetically-thickened eyebrows go up. "Well." Her gaze darts between me, Rory, and the ring. And then they stay on the ring. "*Well.*"

There's a moment of silence. Rory reaches over, grabbing my hand from the armrest of my chair, and holds it, plunking our jointed hands together on the table. The angle is weird, so I shift my grip so our fingers are intertwined. And then, because I can, I bring the back of her hand up to my lips and kiss it.

Rory's eyelashes flutter, and it breaks the spell over the table.

"Well, good," Mrs. Patterson says. "You can start coming by twice a week now. Maybe you can keep Bartholomeow company when I'm at the fitness classes."

"I'm not driving all the way here twice a week just because I'm engaged, Grandma."

"Why? How far away do you live?"

That second question is directed at me.

"About twenty minutes."

Mrs. Patterson points at me and speaks to her granddaughter. "It's not that far once you move in. Twice a week," she insists.

"I'm—I'm not moving in with him," Rory stutters in surprise. Then she backpedals. "Yet, I mean. We're going to wait—"

"Why? You moved at the drop of a hat last time." Mrs. Patterson snaps her fingers. "What, is your fiancé not a good enough reason to move?"

"I moved *for you*."

"Exactly."

"Argh. Grandma, I'm not moving yet."

"Don't be ridiculous. You're going to drive three hours each way every time you want to see your fiancé?"

Three hours? Where the hell does Rory live?

"And," she continues, "I'm not going to have you going out to see him every time you visit and then sneaking in at all hours of the night."

"I won't be sneaking in!"

"Don't you want her to live with you?"

Oh, that's for me.

"Yes, of course," I say. Actually, the thought makes me giddy. I can't even imagine living with her. Does she wear black all the time? Even to bed?

Rory glares at me as if she can read my mind.

I blink at her with faux innocence. "Safety first. Your grandma's right. That's a lot of driving. And what are you going to do in winter?"

Rory points a finger at me. "Don't you dare team up with her."

I gesture to Mrs. Patterson. "She's a smart lady."

Mrs. Patterson preens while her granddaughter grabs one of the many forks set in front of her. I shift my thighs away from her reach.

"I'll think about it," she seethes.

Grandma's Got a Weapon

RORY

Living-situation discussion aside, lunch went about as well as can be expected. Morgan was charming, toeing the line between friendly and flirting, but I'm pretty sure he was doing it just to get a rise out of me.

He smirked at me when the server cleared away all my unused forks.

Now, we're following Grandma upstairs so Morgan can "meet Bartholomeow."

As usual, Grandma is a few paces ahead of me and Morgan falls back to walk beside me.

"I guess we should have seen that moving-in thing coming, huh?"

I blow out a breath. "Yeah."

He's quiet for a few paces, and then asks, "Do you really drive three hours each way?"

"Yup."

"Where do you live?"

"Westchester."

He whistles. "That is far."

"Well, it wasn't far from Grandma two retirement communities ago. She keeps finding reasons to move, though."

He frowns.

"I used to visit once a week. She keeps hating the places." I shrug. "She knew the consequences when she decided to move."

"For what it's worth," he says, leaning in to whisper, "I have a guest bedroom."

I raise an eyebrow. "Are you suggesting I move in?"

"I'm not suggesting anything."

"Well, don't worry, I'm not *actually* moving in."

"I wasn't worried."

We get to Grandma's apartment and she calls for her cat. "Help me find him, Rory."

Grandma goes back to look in her bedroom, and I drop to my knees to look under the couch. Morgan wanders around, looking at Grandma's things.

It's a two-bedroom apartment, with a full kitchen and a balcony. There are pictures everywhere, and I'm in just about all of them.

"Who is this?" Morgan teases, pointing at the picture of me standing at the top of a slide on a playground with a bowl cut when I was about seven. My dad and sister are in the picture too, but in the background. "She looks like a handful."

"You could help, you know."

"I could," he allows. "What does the cat look like?"

I glare at him over my shoulder while I move to look

under the chair. "Why don't you show me any cat you find and I'll tell you if it's the right one."

Morgan laughs.

"Go check on top of the fridge."

He goes around the corner just as Grandma comes back into the room.

I pop my head up. "Did you find him?"

"No. But I have something for you and your fiancé."

"Morgan," I call.

He comes into the living room. Bartholomeow is under Morgan's arm like an awkward football, legs dangling and eyes bewildered. Morgan strokes his head with a finger and Bartholomeow's ears twitch and a low growl emanates from his chest.

"Uhhh . . ." Morgan says. Bartholomeow has decided that his thirty seconds of affection from a stranger are up and launches himself from Morgan's arms and streaks out of the room.

"Well, now you've met him," Grandma remarks, just as she hands me a folded slip of paper.

I glance at Grandma. "What is this?"

She rolls her eyes. "Open it."

Morgan stands at my side and peers over my shoulder as I unfold the paper.

I gasp and quickly fold it again. "Grandma!"

She thumps her cane. "It's for the wedding. Don't cash it until Friday, I have to move some money around."

"Nope," I say, handing it back to her. "We're not having a wedding."

"Like hell you're not."

I shake my head and jut out my chin. "We're getting married at the courthouse. In *a year*."

"Over my dead body! Literally! I could be dead by then."

"We're not going to get married on your timetable just because—"

"You think I'd want to miss your wedding like I missed your—"

"—you've got some morbid obsession with—"

"—parents' then I obviously didn't—"

We both snap our mouths shut when the check is ripped from my hand.

Morgan holds it up. "This is a generous gift, Mrs. Patterson, and Rory and I appreciate the gesture. But if this comes with strings attached, then we don't want it. When and where we get married is entirely up to Rory and me, and we will not tolerate any manipulation on your part, especially if you are going to fight with Rory about every single choice."

Holy shit.

I think my panties just melted.

Grandma stares at Morgan, who stares right back at her as if she's not five whole feet of stubborn, brash, pain-in-the-ass old lady holding a weapon.

He may not realize how effectively she can wield that cane.

"Well," Grandma finally says. She turns to me. "Fine. The money has no strings attached. You can use it for your wedding or your honeymoon or to buy a house right nearby."

Morgan clears his throat.

"Fine. A house anywhere. My lord." She casts a long look at Morgan, and then back to me. "I like him. He's a keeper."

I know, Grandma. I know.

You Win This Time

RORY

EVEN THOUGH HE JUST SAW ME A FEW HOURS AGO, Morgan lights up when I walk into On the Rocks.

I take my seat at the bar and he delivers my beer and then leans against the counter. "So, how much did your grandma love me?"

I take a swig. "She wouldn't stop talking about you."

He fist pumps.

"I knew it. Grandmas like me. Even though yours is particularly prickly. Like someone I know," he teases.

I roll my eyes. "Don't get too excited. She loves me and is still a pain in my ass."

"She's really not too bad." He lifts his chin to indicate behind me. I turn around—the older ladies are back in the corner booth. "The one wearing the 'Queer AF' T-shirt? That's Miss Mullins. She's the nicest lady in the world but she has no filter. Your grandma's like that . . . she says whatever's on her mind. The difference is your grandma's mean."

The woman in question catches us looking at her and waves. Then she picks up her beer bottle and grabs a fork from the basket at the center of the table and starts tapping them together.

Ah, hell no.

I get up out of my seat and stomp over to the table, my hands in my leather jacket. The fancy one's eyebrows have climbed up nearly to her hairline and the other one, the hippie, has shrunk back, casting a nervous glance at Miss Mullins. "We're not performing monkeys. We'll kiss when we want to kiss."

Miss Mullins is undeterred. "It's just harmless wedding fun."

"Do we look like we're at a wedding?"

"Does that mean I can do it at your wedding?"

"You're not in—"

"Okay, now!" Morgan grabs my elbow and tugs me away from the women. "She's not a fan of PDA," he calls back as he pushes me back to my seat. "But I love her anyway!"

I glare at Morgan as he comes around the bar.

"It's just a stupid little thing. I wouldn't have kissed you if you didn't want it. But I would have handled it in a more charming way." He grins.

I open my mouth, about to argue that charm doesn't get you everything, especially, in my experience, with old ladies. Instead, he cuts me off.

"Besides, they think we're getting married and you're going to move here and they just want to get to know you. And, yeah, they probably figured they would be invited to my wedding, since they've known me since I was in diapers."

I make a face. "And you'd invite them?"

"Of course."

I narrow my eyes at him. "How big would our wedding be?"

Morgan leans back against the far counter and crosses an arm over his chest, rubbing his chin with the other. "Well, let's see. Me, you, your grandma, my best friends—that's Kit, Hunter, Silas. They'd get dates. I'd like to invite my uncle who lives in Buffalo and maybe his daughters, since he won't know anyone else and it'd be nice to meet them. The rest of the staff here, like Paul in the back. There are about two thousand Herevians. But," he wobbles his head back and forth. "Then we'd probably have to hold it outside 'cause there isn't a venue nearby that could fit that many people. I'm thinking barbecue catering, sometime in late spring, maybe May? Oh, I bet one of my friends could get ordained and do the service."

Morgan's gaze returns to mine. He leans forward, reaching over the bar, and with a finger under my chin, clicks my mouth closed.

"Hypothetically, of course."

My brain is trying to calibrate some kind of response to the entire planning out of a completely never-going-to-happen wedding in front of me, so it takes me a moment to realize that Morgan's hand hasn't left my face. Instead, his gaze drops to my mouth and his thumb brushes over my bottom lip.

Is he going to kiss me?

No, of course not. Morgan sighs and pulls away. He looks like he's about to say something else when someone calls down the bar for a drink refill, and Morgan gives me a small smile before he walks away.

The wedding plans tumble through my mind as Morgan does his job. What he's describing sounds awful. I can picture the groom's side chock-full of people and on my side just my grandma. Who else am I going to invite? Work colleagues? They live hours away. I wouldn't know anyone at my wedding.

The check Grandma gave me burns a hole in my pocket. It would more than cover an outdoor, barbecue-catered wedding, even for two thousand Herevians. I can't believe Grandma would casually throw so much money at me like that.

Guilt sits deep in my stomach. Obviously, I'm not going to deposit the check. That might be a problem later down the line when she notices the money's still in her account. In all likelihood, I'll be right there with her when she notices, considering we spend time during every single visit reviewing her bank statements.

My tots come out of the kitchen and I juggle them, my beer, and my helmet and head over to an empty booth. I'm tired of people-ing right now, and the anxiety of introducing Grandma to Morgan today has me exhausted.

So exhausted I wolf down my food and then close my check with Morgan.

"Hold up," he says when I've paid. "I'll walk you out." He points to the room with the pool table, where I recognize a few of his friends. "Be right back!" he shouts.

There are whoops, which I choose to ignore.

My bike's right out front, down a few stairs and in the first parking spot. Morgan puts his hands in his pockets. "So, when am I going to see you again?"

"On my regularly scheduled visit, duh."

Morgan laughs. "What, I can't hope that I'll get to see my fiancée more often now?"

"Fake fiancée," I say. When I look up, I'm facing the

bar and the giant windows where several faces now peer out at us. "Fucking hell. We have an audience."

He glances over and whistles. "What did you say earlier? Dancing monkeys?"

"Yeah," I mutter. It would look really weird if I didn't kiss my fiancé goodbye, right?

"If I dipped you and kissed you right now, would you punch me?"

"Probably." I swing my leg over the bike, just to make sure he wasn't seriously considering it.

"Good thing I'll settle for a kiss on the cheek." He turns his back to the window, facing me, his thigh bumping up against my knee. Then he leans in and gently presses the side of his face to mine, barely brushing me. It probably looks like a real kiss to anyone watching. "Drive safe," he whispers, and then backs up.

I ignore the flutters in my stomach and swing my helmet on. Then I fire up the bike and Morgan waves. He watches me pull away.

Small-town people are nosy. When I agreed to this charade, I didn't think about all the people in Morgan's life that we're deceiving.

This isn't what I wanted. When I left Grandma in her sickbed, all I wanted was for us both to be a little less lonely, even if it was only temporary. Agreeing to go out on a date with Morgan is one thing—faking an engagement is another.

How did this get so out of control?

I wonder if he's told his best friends that all this is pretend.

And then I wonder about that wedding he was planning. He was dressed up for lunch today, looking hot as hell. What kind of ridiculous tie would he wear to our wedding?

I have never once thought about wearing a white dress, but stupid Morgan put a seed in my head. I wouldn't want to wear anything long or lacy or with fucking sequins on it.

Morgan probably pictures a bride in a long white dress with a veil or some stupid shit.

Not me.

By the time I trudge up to Grandma's apartment, I'm even crankier than usual. When I turn the corner, though, my mood plummets.

My backpack is sitting outside Grandma's door.

I run down the hallway like two seconds are going to make a goddamn difference in reality and shove my key into the lock. It turns, but when I push it open, Grandma is *right there*, blocking my entrance.

"Grandma," I seethe.

"What?" She's ready for a fight already, I can tell. I consider shouldering my way in, but I don't want to hurt her.

"What is my backpack doing out here?"

"Why do you think? Go back to your fiancé's house and quit bothering me."

"I'm not staying at Morgan's house; I'm staying with you."

"Like hell you are. Good night, Rory. Tell Morgan to wrap it up. Or don't. I'd like great-grand babies."

"Grandma. I'm warning you. Let me in."

She shuts the door on my face.

"Grandma!"

I pound my fist on the wood, which does nothing but hurt my hand.

A door opens down the hall and a frowning old lady sticks her head out.

I bite off a curse and look up at the ceiling. I cannot yell at old ladies in public twice in one day, especially not her neighbors. I need them to like her so she can finally make some fucking friends.

"Fine," I say. "Whatever." We normally have breakfast together before I drive home but just for this, breakfast is off the table. I even consider driving home, but it's been a long day and I don't think I can safely make the drive back. I sling my backpack over my shoulder and stomp down the hallway. I guess I'm going back to the bar. You win this time, Grandma.

Who's My
Good Girl?

RORY

MORGAN'S FACE LIGHTS UP THE MOMENT HE CATCHES SIGHT of me back in his bar. "Miss me already?" he says, leaning his forearms on the bar. He is *fucking delighted* to see me and he doesn't even know the best—or worst—part of it yet.

I toss my backpack on the bar with a thunk. "Grandma kicked me out."

He does a really bad job of hiding his laughter with a cough and I glare at him.

"Shut up. And please tell me you have a guest bed."

"Well . . ." He scratches his cheek and turns, stalling by grabbing my favorite beer from the cooler.

"*Morgan.*"

"I only have one bed. And it's a twin."

His lip twitches. The fucker is lying.

"And I don't own pajamas."

"You're a bad liar," I tell him.

"And the heat is off. We'll have to snuggle for warmth. I bet you're a great cuddler."

"I do not cuddle," I growl. I reach over the bar to smack his shoulder.

Morgan evades me, laughing, and someone else down the bar calls to him for a refill. I swipe my beer off the counter and stalk over to a booth. I read until the bar closes, and then I follow his truck home, wondering what I'm getting myself into.

He lives on one of the streets off Main, in a rustic-looking one-story house with a driveway that runs through the property to a setback garage and a fenced-in backyard. The porch lights are on, but there are no streetlights in this part of town, so most of the house is shrouded in shadows. Morgan drives all the way back and stops in front of the garage, so I park my bike right behind him on the driveway and shut it off. When I pull my helmet off, I hear barking.

Morgan slams his truck door. "Shit, I should have asked. You aren't allergic to dogs? Or afraid of them?"

"No." I eye the house. The barking is loud.

"Good. Okay, come on in."

We enter the backyard first, which triggers a motion sensor light to come on, through the chain-link gate and up to the back porch. "Hang on," he tells me. "I'm going to let her out. Normally when I get home she's sleeping, but your bike must've woken her up and she's all hyper now."

He opens the door and a dog rockets out, smashing into the side of the deck and rebounding to take the stairs in one giant leap and sprint toward me.

"That must've hurt," I say.

"You'd think so, but she does it all the time. Broke the damn thing once."

The dog does a lap, then runs between the two of us, bouncing and cavorting with her tail wagging all over the place. In the harsh floodlight, I can see that she's a golden retriever.

"Rory, meet Princess. Princess, meet Rory."

I stare at Morgan. "Are you fucking kidding me right now? Your dog's name is Princess?"

Morgan kneels down and starts talking to his dog, who couldn't stand still if her life depended on it. "That's because she *is* a princess. Who's my good girl, who's a princess, who's the best dog ever?" He's regressed to baby talking to his dog, but then he looks up at me and says in a normal voice, "Her full name is Princess Buttercup Law, Collector of Tennis Balls and Defender of Pine Lane."

Of course it is.

The dog has calmed down enough to lean against Morgan for butt scratches, momentarily forgetting about me, until she remembers and bounds over again. This time she sniffs circles around me.

"Hi."

She keeps sniffing, finding something particularly interesting on my right boot heel.

I look up at Morgan, who tilts his head at me. "Have you never had a dog?"

"No. No pets except for Bartholomeow, and definitely no dogs."

"Sad," he remarks. "Dogs are the best. Okay, girl, let's go inside."

We step through the back door into a tiled room with a rowing machine and a TV. Morgan leads me into the next room, which is a kitchen-living-room combo that stretches all the way to the front door. There's a small kitchen table in the middle and a tiny alcove to the right.

"Okay, give me a minute to, uh, clean up the guest

bedroom." He grins at me before disappearing into that alcove. I poke my head into it—there's just enough room for three doors: the middle one is half open and reveals a bathroom counter, the left one is closed, and the right one is the one Morgan's in.

Okay, so he does have a guest room. Presumably with a bed.

Why am I disappointed?

Drawers slam and there are thumps that sound an awful lot like cardboard boxes being moved around.

Princess trots after him, tail wagging to see what all the fuss is about, leaving me alone.

I drop my bag on the floor and look around. The big walls have those large frames designed for multiple regular-sized photos in them, and I lean in to take a closer look. There are older pictures that show a young Morgan—no baby or kid photos, but as a teenager. I recognize some of his friends in them. I spot a few pictures set in the bar and a lot of pictures with snow—a chairlift from behind with three bundled-up people; a tailgate party with Morgan, three guys, and two girls; and a picture of the view from the top of a mountain looking down over the snowy land-scape of the town.

There's a framed newspaper clipping too.

SKIING TEENS FIND BURIED SKIER

The story's about a skier who slid off one of the runs the day after a big snowstorm. He got stuck in the powder between the trees and the "local high school boys" found him and dug him out before he suffocated.

"That was wild," Morgan says, coming to stand beside me. "You ever ski?"

"Nope. This calls you a hometown hero."

Morgan shrugs. "Eh. I found the guy. Hunter had the shovel. Your room is ready."

I turn to follow him into the bedroom. Boxes are piled up on one side, but the full-sized bed is clear and is made up with sheets and a comforter. It's not a big room, but it's just me and a backpack.

And a dog, apparently, who jumps up on the bed.

"Hey, Princess, get down from there."

She obeys, only to put her chin on the edge of the bed and wag her tail while staring up at us.

"Okay, that's my room across the hall"—he points to the left door—"and this is the bathroom." He pushes the middle door open and shows me the sink, toilet, and shower.

I walk in and look around.

Morgan leans on the doorframe, one elbow resting on the wood above his head. His bicep is obscene. "Help yourself to anything you need. Towels in there, shampoo's in the shower. I, uh, don't get up early in the morning since I work late, so help yourself to anything in the kitchen too."

"Yeah, okay. Thanks for letting me stay."

"You're welcome. Shout when you're done in the bathroom and I'll take my turn." He taps the top of the doorframe and leaves me to it.

I don't have much with me, since I keep essentials at Grandma's house and she didn't bother to pack them up for me. I find a new toothbrush under the sink and use Morgan's toothpaste. Then I shower, and I haven't showered in a man's bathroom in a long time. It's so . . . utilitarian.

I wrap a towel around my body and one around my hair and then I poke around. Curious about the man I'm "engaged" to.

No medications, no sign of a woman. He's a hometown hero with a fucking golden retriever named Princess.

I exit the bathroom and startle when I spot Morgan sitting on the couch. Princess is wedged into the cushion next to him, belly-up while he strokes her fur. Her lips have succumbed to gravity and she gives me a toothy grin.

The overhead lights are off and there's just the lamp on next to Morgan. The wood floor gleams and the couch looks soft and inviting.

Morgan's smile is as slow as molasses while he looks me over. "Feeling better?"

Am I? I was cranky earlier, pissed at Grandma and annoyed at the locals. Now, after a hot shower and just the right amount of affection from a man and a dog, I feel a lot better.

Tired though.

I nod. "Thanks again."

"Of course. Good night, my queen."

Two Lovebirds

Morgan

I wake up to hot breath on my face. Sadly it smells like dog food, so it's not Rory's.

God, how fucking hot would it have been if she had crawled into bed with me last night? I listened with half an ear for any signs of it happening, but it was dead quiet in my house.

Well, except for Princess's light snoring. And now she's breathing in my face and her tail is whacking into the wood of my nightstand.

"Go back to sleep," I moan. I have blackout curtains in my room to help me sleep better, so I roll over and pull the comforter over my head.

But then I hear the clank of plates in the kitchen and sit bolt upright. Rory's awake.

Princess's tail whacks harder and she whines.

"Yeah okay, fine. I'm up."

I throw a shirt on with my boxers and exit my bedroom. Rory's at the stove, dressed in dark jeans and a tight black long-sleeve shirt. It smells like eggs and butter, and something's steaming on the burner.

"Good morning," I say.

Rory spins around. Her hair's loose and a tangled mess around her face and she glares at me. One hand points at the coffee maker. "Help."

I shuffle past her and let Princess out into the backyard. "It's broken," I say apologetically when I turn around. "I've got instant."

She blanches, but pulls out a coffee mug and fills it with water before putting it in the microwave.

"How'd you sleep?" I ask.

"Fine."

"You driving back home today?"

"Yeah."

Princess is back at the door, so I let her in and feed her. When I turn around, there's a plate of food at the kitchen table.

"Eat." Rory points.

Being monosyllabic is impressive. I sit and eat. The microwave beeps, Rory mixes in the instant coffee and slurps some down.

She grimaces, but then gulps down more.

I make a note to buy better coffee. I don't have it at home often. I'm more likely to grab a cup at Sweet Persuasions while on my morning walk with Princess.

Besides, I don't *need* caffeine to get my day started. Unlike some people, apparently.

Rory finishes her mug while she makes a second plate of food and sits across from me when it's done. On a normal day, she's pretty intimidating, but first thing in the morning, Rory scares even me.

But she's wearing my ring, and all of this—her even being here, let alone wearing my ring and cooking me breakfast—makes me warm and fuzzy inside.

We eat in silence, but I keep sneaking glances at Rory, and I catch her doing it a few times to me. I'm not sure what my hair looks like—I haven't even glanced in the mirror yet—but whatever she sees, she must like, because her cheeks get gradually pinker and pinker.

When we're done, I clean up the kitchen while she packs, and then I walk her out to her bike.

"You gonna see your grandma this morning?"

She snorts. "After she kicked me out last night? Hell no."

"Eh, don't stay mad at her for too long. I liked having you here last night. You should at least stop by since you're so close."

"Yeah, maybe—" She stops. "Do you hear that?"

Someone's singing Chappell Roan's "Hot to Go."

They come into view and it's Miss Mullins singing out loud, dance moves and all. She spots us in the driveway. "Good morning! Oh, look at you two lovebirds." She marches in place, still dancing. "I heard you were at the bar late last night, Rory. So glad we're gonna see more of you around town. Have a great day!"

Rory gawks after her. "I was so mean to her yesterday."

"Are you kidding? She was our sixth-grade teacher. Everyone was a little shit to her at some point."

She sighs and then climbs on her bike.

"I'll see you next time, yeah?"

"Next time," she echoes. She pulls on her helmet, fires up her engine, and roars out of my driveway.

She Called
Me Babe

Morgan

I'M GOING TO NEED SOME BACKUP.

Now that selling Grandma's ring is pushed off to be a Future Morgan problem, I need to finally get my butt in gear about getting the money my brother owes me. It's been a few days since Rory stayed the night at my place. Unfortunately, I've been busy and had to spend a bit of money, just in case she stays again. Leo and Kit helped me clean up my guest bedroom and I found a used coffee maker on one of the online marketplaces. I didn't spend so much that I can't afford groceries or rent, but I'm not able to put away as much as I normally do into the bar fund.

Hence, my need to collect from my brother.

Texting and calling haven't been working. My mom is no help. So it looks like I'm going to have to go in person, which I hate doing.

Visiting my brother is like looking at myself in an alternate universe. This is what I could have become if only I'd been born first, or been Mom's favorite, or hadn't had anywhere else to go.

And maybe it's also a bit of guilt too. Because I'm nothing like my mom. And Graham is just like her.

So the next question is, who do I take for backup? I quickly toss out the idea of anyone in my friend group. Graham hates them all, especially Hunter, who punched Graham the last time I saw him—trust me, he deserved it. Bailey could talk circles around my brother since he's dumber than rocks, but I don't want to bring her to my brother's house. Silas and her brother would kill me.

Which pretty much leaves Rory, and the more I think about it the more I warm up to the idea. My brother would find her hot or intimidating, but either way, I'm certain Rory could handle herself.

I text her, and her instant response cracks me up. I can picture her fake irritated face perfectly.

MY QUEEN

Hey, you have a minute?

No.

Pretty please?

Ugh, fine. But only for you. What?

Can I call you?

What are you a boomer?

Fine.

I call her and explain the situation.

"Let me get this straight," she says. "You want me to go with you to your brother's house—a small-time petty drug dealer—and help get the money he owes you."

"Yeah. He might not have the cash, but at this point I'll take anything of value."

"Should I, like, steal something while you distract him?"

"What? No."

"Do I need to bring a weapon?" Okay, *now* I can hear the barest hint of humor in her voice and I know she's just fucking with me.

"Absolutely not, we're just—"

"Fine, I'm in, whatever."

Well, that was too easy. And now I'm having second thoughts. Rory sounds excited about the danger, and thinking about her with a weapon . . .

Huh. I'm turned on. How 'bout that.

But I also want to spend more time with Rory and get the money. Two birds, one stone. I push the concern away. "Great."

"How do we want to play this? Good cop/bad cop? Should I play the dumb bimbo or the bitchy badass?"

"How is bitchy badass different from your regular self? And also, can we someday role-play you as a dumb bimbo?"

"Rude," she says, but it's half-hearted. "And no."

"When can you come out?"

We pencil in Tuesday afternoon, pending Hunter taking over the bar for me. Normally Rory leaves Here in her rearview mirror headed off to wherever Monday morning, so I'm thrilled that she's going to hang around another day for me.

"By the way, my grandma wants your phone number," she adds.

"Yeah? You can give it to her."

I can't see Rory's face, but I can feel the suspicion over the line. "She wouldn't say why she wants it. And honestly, I'm not sure I want you two conspiring."

"Oh, I know why she wants it."

"You do? Why?"

Rory's gonna be mad. "I sent her flowers."

She gasps. "You did not."

"Yup. The card thanked her for kicking you out."

"Fuuuuuuucccckkkkk," she groans. "You asshole. I'm never going to be able to sleep there again."

I just grin.

"Why am I helping you?"

"Because you secretly like me. And you feel bad that I'm pretending to be engaged to you so you figure you owe me a favor."

"Oh I do?"

"Absolutely. Help me with this and we'll call it even."

"I'll call it even for the fake fiancé bit, but I'm going to get you back for those flowers, Morgan."

And with that ominous warning, Rory hangs up on me.

RORY'S MOTORCYCLE ROARS INTO MY DRIVEWAY RIGHT ON time Tuesday afternoon. I haven't seen her since the night she stayed over.

Princess barks once and then wags her tail.

"Sorry, girl, you're staying behind today." My heart races as I lock the door behind me with both excitement over seeing my pretend fiancée and nerves for trying to squeeze money out of my brother.

I stride out to meet Rory, who kills her engine and

takes her helmet off, but doesn't dismount. Her hair is in those two braids again and she's wearing her leather jacket over a white, tight top.

Watching Rory on a bike is pretty goddamn hot.

She reaches behind her and unlatches a second helmet. "Here."

I stare at it. "We're taking your bike?"

She shrugs. "Sure. Why not? Unless you don't like motorcycles."

"You do realize that your ass plus my crotch plus vibrations equals boners, right?"

She rolls her eyes. "Get on, loser."

Rory always seems to think I'm joking. "Did you just quote *Mean Girls* to me? That's a hidden depth I didn't know you had in you."

Rory ignores me and puts her helmet on, and I follow suit. The engine starts up.

"Can you hear me?" Rory's voice comes in through the helmet as I sling my leg over the backseat.

"A headset? Cool. Uh . . . how should I hold on?"

Rory reaches back, grabbing both my arms and pulling them around her waist, bringing my chest flush with her back.

Awesome.

"Move with me, okay? When I lean, you lean."

I sing the chorus to "Da' Dip" by Freak Nasty but replace the word *dip* with *lean*. Rory ignores me and backs us out the driveway.

"Any instructions for me in front of your brother?" she asks. "Am I your fiancée?"

I think about it. "We might as well call you my fiancée. But don't wear the ring."

"It's in my pocket already. I take it off when I'm wearing my gloves."

Talking is good. It distracts me from thinking about my arms around Rory, her ass nestled into my crotch. "Other than that . . . I don't know what to expect, really. He won't want to pay me, and will insist that he doesn't have the money, but maybe I can get a couple thousand out of him at least."

It's wishful thinking. But I won't know until I try.

The headsets make it easy to tell her where we're going, and for the most part, I get to enjoy the feel of Rory in my arms and the thrill of riding a motorcycle. It'll take us about an hour of back-road driving to get to my brother's place. I don't know why he moved all the way out here, and I don't think I want to know. The nearby town is bigger, but it doesn't have the economy that Here gets thanks to the ski resort, and it's run-down and tired.

Rory's a confident driver, but my heart lurches with every bend in the road and it seems like we're screaming along well above the speed limit, though Rory swears we're not.

The conversation does cease, so I'm left to my own thoughts, which are *wild*. Can you have sex on a motorcycle? Would the vibrations travel up my dick, turning it into a vibrator? I should run an experiment. If only I had a willing test subject . . .

There's no need to announce ourselves when we pull up to the ramshackle place my brother calls home. The bike is loud enough that he comes out, slamming the screen door behind him.

He can't tell it's me until I dismount and take my helmet off. Graham smirks. "What the fuck, Morgan? Riding bitch? I knew it."

I ignore my brother's jab. "Hey, Graham, good to see you."

Rory takes her helmet off and my brother's smile turns

appreciative. "What's a girl like you doing with a guy like my brother?"

I sigh. "Graham, this is my fiancée, Rory."

Rory offers him a chin lift.

"Nice. When's the big day?"

"We haven't decided yet." Actually, that gives me an idea. "Weddings are expensive, man. Gotta collect my money."

My brother's eyes turn sharp. "I ain't got no money for you. But I can hook you up for the bachelor party. Or bachelorette party."

Rory ignores him and wanders over to the other side of her bike, leaning down to check something. Or maybe she's faking it and my brother's making her nervous. Unease slips through me, and I wonder if bringing her was a mistake.

"It's been two years, Graham. You were supposed to pay me back in six months."

I know he's got money. He does have a regular job on top of whatever dumbass stuff he does on the side, plus a nice new truck. And the money was for a dispensary that he never opened.

We argue for a while, and then my phone buzzes in my pocket and I check it.

My Queen

Say $12,000 and act like you don't want it.

I look around. I don't see Rory anywhere. What the hell is she talking about?

I respond with a thumbs-up emoji, though, and she must have been waiting for it, because ten seconds later her voice calls out, "Hey. What's the deal with this?"

Graham and I both turn. Rory's next to the garage, lifting a cover on an old SUV. The grass has grown up around it and the paint is an ugly brown color.

My brother shrugs. "I've had it for a while, just been sitting there."

"Does it run?"

"I start it up every few months."

Rory contemplates the vehicle and then glances up at me. "Babe, you know my nephew needs a ride. Maybe your brother could offer you a good deal on this one and you can forgive some of his debt. Since he's not using it."

Babe. She called me *babe.* Sure, it's an act for my brother but I'll take it.

Also . . . she has a nephew?

"You want your nephew to drive that thing? It's a piece of shit. And just because Graham starts it up every so often doesn't mean it runs well."

"I didn't think you'd want a car," my brother interjects. "But maybe your Rory has a good idea here."

Rory takes the cover completely off. It's . . . not an attractive vehicle. Graham obviously doesn't have the cash, so he'd rather give me a piece-of-shit instead. Fuck knows what I'm gonna do with this thing, but I trust Rory.

"That isn't gonna pay for our wedding, *babe.* We need cash."

Rory puts her hands on her hips and scrunches up her face. "What do you think this is worth, anyway?"

I make an exaggerated sigh. "I don't know. Maybe twelve thousand?"

My brother starts walking to the SUV, shaking his head. "Look, since you're my brother and you did lend me money, I can go as low as fourteen."

"Twelve." Rory stands firm. "*If* it can make it home."

My brother rubs his chin and I hold my breath. Will he

think it's worth it to get me to stop bugging him? I'm skeptical, because what incentive does he have to give me anything?

Finally, he drops his hand. "Keys are in the glove box."

Uh-oh. Maybe this really *is* a piece-of-shit. Have I just traded part of the debt my brother owes me for nothing?

Rory opens the door and slides in. It starts on the second try, sputtering and coughing for a good thirty seconds.

"I don't know, Rory . . ."

"They don't make them like this anymore, you know. Your girl has a good eye."

Jesus. My brother can really blow smoke when he wants to. He doesn't know shit about cars.

Rory gets out, leaving the door open and one boot on the floorboard. "Please, *babe*. It would make my niece so happy."

"I thought it was your nephew?" My brother's eyes narrow.

"One of each," Rory says smoothly.

"Whatever. Do we have a deal?"

I genuinely have no idea what's happening here. But Rory looks at me, her eyes begging me, and maybe it's not an act.

"Fine." I cross my arms and scowl like I am *not* happy about it.

My brother disappears to get a bill of sale and Rory digs the title out of the glove box too. Signatures are collected and the next thing I know, I'm driving this clunker home, Rory's motorcycle roaring behind me.

Netflix and
Chill

RORY

MORGAN'S DRIVEWAY IS CROWDED WITH HIS TRUCK, THE Bronco, and my bike. As soon as I pull my helmet off, he runs his hand through his hair and stares at the Bronco. "Care to explain to me why I just drove this clunker home?"

I run my hand over hood and pat it. "Ignore him. He knows not what he speaks of."

"Are you talking to it?" He's amused now. Inside the house, Princess barks at us, and her head pops up in the den window, tail wagging behind her and a dopey doggy grin on her face.

I turn and rest my hip on the hood. Riding with Morgan behind me was distracting. But he was warm and hard and I liked the way his arms felt around my waist. When we drove away from his brother's place, him in the

Bronco, me on the bike, I had to shake off the disappointment and the cold on my back. "Do you know what kind of car this is?"

He walks over to the back. "A Ford."

"Right, but what model?"

He squints. "I don't know. It looks like maybe there used to be something here but it popped off." He points at a spot on the paint front of the passenger door.

"Yeah. It's suspicious as hell, but also, your brother's a fucking idiot."

Morgan glances at me. "No argument there, but I'm feeling like a bit of an idiot here too."

"Well, here's a lesson that I'm pretty sure I don't have to teach you because you aren't *that* dumb: know what you have before you sell it. And in the spirit of that, I'll tell you what exactly you have here before you sell it to me."

His eyebrows rise.

I look down at the shitty paint job in an ugly color that someone's going to hell for inflicting upon this beautiful machine. "This is a first-generation Ford Bronco. They built about two hundred thousand of them in the sixties and seventies, but this one is a Roadster body style. There were only about five thousand of them made from '66 to '68. This is the one collectors look for." I look up at Morgan, who's standing stock still with wide eyes. "I'll buy half of it from you for eleven grand plus twenty-five percent of whatever profit I make from it." I take a deep breath. "I haven't looked closely at the interior and I have no idea if I'll be able to get the parts I need to fix it up properly. Yes, it's barely worth anything *now*. But we could get sixty grand or so when I'm done with it."

He stares at me. "Holy shit." He spins around, stalking off and tugging at his hair. "Holy shit," he says again. "Do you think my brother knew what he had? He had to have, right?"

"There's no way anyone who's even remotely into cars would sell this thing."

"Yeah, but it needs work. I wouldn't know the first thing about how to fix it up. Maybe it wouldn't sell for that much in this condition."

"You're right, it wouldn't. Do you think your brother cares about that?"

Morgan runs his hand down his face. "Fuck. Okay. Fuck."

I laugh, giddy with the idea of owning this beast. Also, catching Morgan off guard is hilarious. He's usually so confident and in control, but now he's flustered, which means the tables have turned. I think about how I felt when he was half naked and dancing up against me, and this kind of revenge is pretty sweet.

"Stop it," Morgan chides, and that throws a bucket of cold water over me.

I press my lips tight.

He continues, "Okay, look, I'll gladly sell it to you for whatever you want. How are you going to get it home?"

Oh, right. I consider this problem. "Can I leave it here for a few days?"

"Yeah sure." He pauses and eyes the Bronco cautiously. "My brother might figure all this out."

"Do you think he might try to steal it back?"

Morgan shakes his head. "I don't know." His head falls back to look up at the sky. The daylight is just starting to fade. "Why don't we put it in my garage for now?"

First, Morgan lets Princess out into the backyard, and I reach over the chain-link fence to give her a head pat. Then Morgan opens the garage door manually. It isn't hoarding-level full, but there are boxes and lawn equipment and things for Princess.

"I guess I'll put cleaning this place on my project list," Morgan says. "For now, let's just see how much of it we can move to the side."

I start moving boxes, and Morgan picks up loose things and piles them on a table in the back. I hear a faint buzzing sound, and Morgan pats his pocket. He pulls out his phone, checks the screen, and then ignores the call.

"So, how did you know about the Bronco, uh . . ."

"Roadster."

"Yeah, that one."

"I've always been into cars. And bikes, too."

Morgan looks out the garage door at my motorcycle. "I've always wondered if you had another ride."

"I do. A Honda Civic."

He stops, a pair of pliers in his hand. "A souped-up Civic?"

I roll my eyes. "No, I'm more into classics. My Civic is factory standard."

"Do you work with cars? Like for your job? Since I don't know what you do," he teases.

I still haven't told Morgan what I do. It used to be because I didn't want to bother making a friend just to lose them when Grandma moves again. And then it was just fun to see the kind of guesses he could come up with.

In general, I don't often tell guys what I do. I get a variety of responses that usually all boil down to men not being able to handle a woman in a "man's job." Same with rebuilding cars.

But now . . .

"I work in robotics."

He straightens. "No shit, really?"

"Yeah. I work as a service technician for a firm in

Boston. I handle most of the lower New England area, fixing things when shit breaks or helping set up new systems."

Morgan whistles. "A smart technician and a car aficionado." His gaze is warm, looking at me like I can take on the world, and my heart kicks hard. A man who likes a woman's competence is hot. "How's your grandma like all that?"

I smile down at the box in my arms as I move it to the back. "She bought me my first car when I was fourteen." I set the box on top of another one and pause, thinking about that car. "A Jaguar E-Type. Even worse off than this one." I lift my chin to the Bronco. "Took me eight years to rebuild it. When I sold it I tried to give her the money and she told me to 'accept the damn gift.' I've been looking for another project ever since."

My eyes meet Morgan's across the garage. "I already knew you were a badass," he says, and the warmth and affection in it makes me realize that Morgan being my friend isn't a lie anymore.

It takes an hour for us to clear space for the Roadster. Morgan's phone rings twice more, and he ignores the call, despite me telling him I've got this. "How did my brother come to own this car anyway, without knowing what it was?" Morgan asks once I pull it into the garage.

I cringe, hearing the engine echo in the small space. I quickly turn it off and hop out. "It's rare, but it happens. People, especially in rural areas, tend to keep cars just lying around, and then the owners die or forget about them. There was a story a few years ago about a woman who passed away, and her kids discovered a Ferrari and a Lamborghini in the garage. *Two supercars.* I can't imagine buying this beauty and then forgetting about it."

"Well, I'm glad it's ours now."

I glance at him, wondering if it feels weird to him too to say that something belongs to the both of us. His arms are crossed, and there's dust in his hair. The sunlight outside is dying, and the harsh lights of the garage make his face look more angular.

I shake the attraction away. "There's a couple more things I want to do," I say. "Then I better head out so I can get home in a reasonable time."

"Yeah, sure. Need any help?"

"Nah, go inside. I'll be there in a few."

Morgan leaves, and this next bit gets messy. I take one of the tires off and hide it behind boxes. I pull the spark plugs and drain the engine oil.

Just in case.

We had to shuffle the vehicles around to get the Bronco in the garage, so my motorcycle is out on the street. I put one of the keys in the rear storage space under my seat, just in case.

I head back into the house to say goodbye. I can hear Morgan talking, so I toe off my boots by the front door and follow the sound of his voice.

He's in the den, the room right off the back door. He's talking to someone on the phone, and Princess's head rests on his knee while he absentmindedly pets her. The dog's eyes rise to look at me in the doorway, but Morgan's not paying attention.

"Yeah, Mom, I know."

I freeze. Morgan's voice is tinged with sadness and frustration. His shoulders are up around his ears.

"He owed me—"

I can't tell what his mom is saying, but she's loud and upset, not letting Morgan finish his sentence.

"Mom—"

The more the woman yells, the more hunched over

Morgan gets. His hand leaves Princess's head only to pinch the bridge of his nose.

I slowly back away and retreat to the living room.

I don't have many memories of my parents. I'm sure there were tough moments, but the memories I do have are all good ones.

Not like this.

No wonder Morgan is so close to his friends. No wonder he's so friendly with everyone in town. All the Herevians he's known his whole life, they're his real family.

"Hey," Morgan says as he enters the room, Princess at his heels. "You headed out?"

He's smiling, but it doesn't quite reach his eyes now.

I hate it. I hate it so much that an excuse to leave isn't what comes out when I open my mouth.

"Wanna order a pizza?"

His whole face lights up.

"We could watch a movie too," I add.

"Oh Rory," he teases, grabbing his phone out of his back pocket and the remote from the coffee table. "I would love to Netflix and chill with you."

Another Lie

Morgan

Rory resting her head against my shoulder is the most exciting thing that's happened to me all day—yeah, more than discovering I practically robbed my brother and got Rory her dream car—until I realize she's asleep.

Did I intentionally pick a super long movie so that it would be too late for her to ride home at the end?

Maybe.

But I genuinely did not expect her to fall asleep in the middle of it.

There's an empty pizza box on the coffee table, and Rory's boots and jacket are on the floor and rack, respectively, by the front door. I had pulled out a blanket, hoping for a cuddling opportunity, but Rory'd tucked herself into a cocoon.

And then Princess had sat on her other side, and I

didn't have the heart to kick her off when Rory started petting her.

After an exciting day, I guess it's no surprise she was tired. Slumped against me, she's soft and warm. She smells good too, something that's not floral but nutty and creamy.

I let her snooze on my shoulder until the credits roll, and then I carefully turn sideways, keeping her head on my shoulder but shifting so I can get my arms under her and pick her up.

She grunts, and I stand in the middle of my living room holding her until she settles down. She's warm and dead weight in my arms, and I like it.

I like the domesticity, too. In another world, where Rory was my girlfriend, I'd carry her to my bed. I'd wake her up with tender kisses and exploring hands, and she'd let me in.

Instead, Rory's my fake fiancée.

Princess hops off the couch and follows me into Rory's room.

I carefully set Rory down on the bed, her head on a pillow, but she immediately shifts and stretches, blinking up at me.

"Did I fall asleep?"

"Yeah. Go back to sleep."

She sighs, but then sits up, her eyes barely slitted open. "Have to pee."

I let Princess out for her bathroom break too, and when I come inside, I hear the sounds of Rory brushing her teeth. I change into my sleep clothes and linger in the hallway.

When the door opens, she's just as bleary-eyed as before, but now she's pantsless. My gaze travels down from her tight black T-shirt to her matching underwear and socks. "Bed" is all she says. She leaves the door open as she climbs onto the bed and under the covers.

The bedside lamp is still on, and she makes no move to turn it off. She might be asleep again already.

I tiptoe in and click the light off myself. I'm about to pull the door shut behind me when Rory calls out, "Morgan?"

"Yeah?" I swing the door back open enough to poke my head in.

"Thanks for making my room prettier," she mumbles into her pillow.

I smile in the dark. "You're welcome. Good night, Rory."

IN THE MORNING, I'M AWAKENED BY A PHONE BLARING somewhere inside my house. I hear a hushed voice and Princess, sleeping next to me on the bed, grumbles.

"I know," I tell her, sitting up. "But it's Rory. Her sleep schedule is different from ours."

But I'm not going to miss out on a chance to spend time with her. Plus I feel like if I don't get up she might sneak off without saying goodbye.

Princess reluctantly follows me, and whatever feelings she has about getting up early must not be too bad because her tail goes bananas behind her when she spots Rory at the kitchen table on the phone.

"Good morning," I call out.

Rory's eyes widen and she puts a finger to her lips. "Grandma, don't worry about it." She listens for a beat and then rubs the space between her eyebrows. "God, no,

Grandma. Jesus. I'm not cheating on Morgan. It is Morgan, okay?"

I grab the phone from Rory and ignore her protests. "Good morning, Mrs. Patterson. Lovely day out today, isn't it?"

"I don't need to hear all about your good morning," she snaps. "Are you at her place or your place?"

Rory tries to swipe for the phone. "My place," I answer.

"Good. Has she moved in with you yet?"

"I'm working on it."

"Well try harder. I need help with my computer this week."

"I could come help you."

"It's personal. Banking stuff. You're not trusted until you lock her down, understand?"

"Yes, ma'am. I'm working on that too."

She harrumphs. "Put my granddaughter back on the phone."

I hand the phone over and listen to one side of an argument about where Rory should live. Rory's losing.

"I haven't moved to Here because *you* can't make up your mind about where to live. . . . I've moved three times for you! . . .You can't stay here because of me. You'll be miserable again in two months. . . . Because I know you, that's why! . . . Fine," Rory finally snaps. "I'll move. Are you happy now?"

Once Mrs. Patterson achieves victory, the call is short. Rory hangs up and glares at her phone.

"So your grandma moves a lot?"

Rory huffs. "She's hated every place she's lived in so far. She wants to live with me, but I'm home so rarely. I sleep in hotels more often than I sleep at home. Actually, I sleep at Grandma's more than I sleep at home."

"It does make sense for you to move then."

"I'm not really moving," she says. "How would she know, anyway?"

"Another lie?" I tsk at her. Princess whines by the door so I get up and let her out into the backyard.

Rory makes a face. "What Grandma doesn't know doesn't hurt her. Just told her I'd move; I didn't say *when*."

Are You Stalking Me?

FRIDAY MORNING I HAVE A CLEANING JOB WITH KIT. IT'S one of the regular ones, not a show, so Kit and I buckle down with a little less fanfare and a little more chit chat.

"How are things going with Rory?"

Kit's the only one who knows that this engagement isn't real, but he also knows that I am totally into Rory.

I think about my words carefully. "It's slow going. But we're spending more time together. Last week she fell asleep on my shoulder when we were watching TV."

Kit gasps. "The scandal."

"Shut it," I say. We're cleaning the kitchen right now, so I'm tackling the dirty dishes the vacationers left behind and Kit's cleaning the stove. "She's just . . . it's hard to get her to open up."

"Yeah." Kit scoffs. "Classic avoidant type."

"Avoidant type?"

"Yeah, everyone has an attachment type. Like their childhood affects how they treat relationships now."

"What attachment type are you? Desperate?"

"Ha ha. There's three types: secure, insecure"—he glances at me pointedly—"and avoidant. Alex is avoidant too."

Alex is Kit's best friend—well, his other best friend. Kit went to college and they were roommates their freshman year. As it tends to happen when one goes off to college, Kit and I didn't keep in touch like we used to, and at the time, it was hard for me. I was already feeling the sting of being left behind, and then to have Kit choose to work in Albany for a while after college hurt. And *then*, when he quit his job, he worked on Alex's farm for a few months before coming back home.

I have a lot of complicated feelings around this—the lack of funds to go to college or even to get away from Here didn't help. But now I'm glad I didn't, and Kit's back, so our friendship is back and stronger than ever.

"How'd you break through to Alex?"

Kit pauses. "Mostly I hugged him until he gave in. So, smother her with affection?"

I put the last plate in the dish drain. "Already do that."

Kit screws up his face. "Well, alcohol probably helped too. A few nights wasted and a few days hungover really cement a friendship."

"You're not helpful at all."

He shrugs and tosses his cleaning rag in the laundry pile. "I can't help that I'm more lovable than you." He puts his hands on his hips. "We done here?"

I turn off the water and put the sponge in the trash, the sink now sparkling clean. "Yup."

"Good, we need to talk."

Now it's my turn to mock gasp. "Are you firing me?"

"No, but let's sit down."

Kit digs around in his backpack and pulls out a manila folder, the likes of which I haven't seen since the bar's hiring process went digital ages ago.

He joins me at the dining room table and pulls one piece of paper out. "This is a nondisclosure agreement. My dad looked it over and says it's all pretty standard. I need you to sign it for the job tomorrow."

"Mysterious," I say, and sign the paper, because Kit's dad is a lawyer and I trust him.

Kit puts the paper back in the folder and leans in. "Wednesday, we're going to do the Cosmopolitan package for none other than—"

What?

Did you think I was going to *tell you*? I *just* signed an NDA. Nice try.

Kit drops me home after our talk and I'm instantly on alert. There's an unmarked van outside my curb, and Princess does not greet me at the door.

The van is probably nothing—a neighbor having a handyman swing by or a friend visiting. Princess's absence could mean one of two things. She could have escaped. Unlikely, but possible. The second option is more likely, though.

She's gotten herself in trouble.

More than once I've come home to find Princess hiding because she's made a mess. Twice I discovered she'd stolen food off the counter. Once she accidentally closed herself in the guest bedroom. And *three times* I came home and she'd gotten her head stuck in the lid of the trash can.

I have a different style of trash can now, so I'm wondering if she ate a loaf of bread off the counter—plastic and all (it's happened before).

I step inside the back room and hear Princess scrambling from wherever she was.

"Owwwww," a voice says.

Princess didn't grow a magical voice box. My dog bounds through the house, her whole body wriggling in pure joy. She looks up at me, prancing in place, while I begin toeing off my shoes, and then she darts away, back to the rest of the house. When I take too long, dropping my keys on the table and hanging my jacket up, Princess reappears at the doorway again wearing a concerned expression. *Dad, are you coming? Dad? Dad!*

She disappears again, and a moment later she whimpers.

Then I hear, "Don't come whining to me, you're the one that got off the couch. I was comfortable."

There's another whine.

When I step into the main room, I see black jeans and socked feet crossed at the ankle on my couch. Rory's lying there, her laptop half open on the coffee table.

"Fine," Rory says, and Princess leaps onto Rory's stomach, which causes her to grunt and push my dog off. Princess burrows into the space between Rory and the back cushion while Rory chuckles.

"Well, hello." I saunter into the living room.

Princess's tail *thump thump thump*s and she whines in pleasure.

I lean over the couch, putting one fist above Rory's head on the arm of the couch and the other fist on the back, caging my two girls in.

"Are you stalking me?" I ask. "If so, I'm into it."

Rory rolls her eyes. "I was driving through and I stopped to visit Grandma and wanted to talk to you. And check on the car."

Sure, check on "the car."

"You weren't home," she continues with a how-dare-you tone. "So I waited on the porch. And Princess heard me and she was whining and I couldn't just sit there while she was all alone so I went to your back door and found the key under the mat—not very secure by the way—and thought I'd wait for you inside. Keep her company, you know." Rory sniffs as if she's done me a favor.

"Uh-huh," I say. "How long did you last before you decided you'd rather do a B and E than listen to Princess cry?"

The dog in question squirms. She's lying on Rory's arm, which has got to be numb by now. Princess wiggles her way up to Rory's face and gives her cheek a lick before she tucks her nose behind Rory's neck.

"Twenty minutes."

"Liar."

"Fine. Seven. But I—"

Whatever Rory is about to say is cut off by Princess's giant sneeze. Rory's whole face contorts into a half grimace, half wince, and I'm sure she's got dog snot all over the back of her neck and in her hair.

"That," I say to Princess, "was disgusting. Did no one teach you that it's impolite to sneeze on guests?" I reach up to the side table and grab a tissue, offering it to Rory. "Need this?"

An eye cracks open and Rory glares at me. She moves to sit up and there's a scramble while Princess ungracefully gets to her feet and leaps over Rory.

"So you wanted to talk to me?" I settle my butt on the

coffee table while Rory wipes the dog snot off the back of her neck.

"Yeah." She sighs. "Grandma is calling our bluff. She wants to come see my 'new place' and have dinner with us."

"Sure, no problem."

Rory's hand drops. "Morgan. That means I'd have to actually move stuff in here. My grandmother will be coming over and she'll snoop."

I spread my hands wide. "So move in. It's not like we have to share a bed. We'll make it look believable and then after she leaves you can move back into the guest room. And look, you travel a lot, I work nights, we'll hardly ever see each other."

"Right," she says slowly. "And I don't know how long we'll need to keep this up. In two months or so, Grandma's going to insist on moving again."

"Exactly. No big deal."

Rory blows out a breath. "That means I need to *actually move* here. I figured since you're off on Monday we could have dinner then, but that only gives me two days to move in, and I need someone to come with me and drive my car and the van back. And you've got work. Although . . ." She pauses, thinking. "I can't fit all of my stuff in my car anyway."

I pull out my phone. "Think my truck would have enough room? You wouldn't need to bring furniture, right? Just your personal stuff?" She agrees. "Okay, let me rally the troops and see who can help." I fire off a text to my friends and stand. "Has Princess been out?"

Rory nods. "When I got here."

"Have you eaten?"

Rory shakes her head.

By the time I've made sandwiches and we sit down to

eat, the group chat has coordinated. "Right, so, tomorrow morning Bailey, Silas, and Kit will swing by and we'll take my truck to your place. Load the cars up, I'll drive your car back here, Kit will drive your van, you ride the bike, and Bailey and Silas will bring my truck back. That'll get me back in time to open the bar at four."

Rory thinks about it. "Aren't you closing the bar tonight?"

"I'll let Silas drive my truck in the morning and I'll sleep in the passenger side."

"Where will I park?"

I'm not sure if she's talking about her bike, car, or van, so I answer for all three. "Why don't you park your work van on the street, and the bike in the grass by the driveway. Then we only have to worry about shuffling your car and my truck."

Rory nods, and then Princess bounds up and nudges Rory for head rubs. Rory bends down. "You're going through an awful lot of trouble for me."

"You are trouble," I say, and the quick half smile on her face tells me she takes it as the compliment I intended. A thought occurs to me and I snap my fingers. "Or, you could stay here tonight and ride with us tomorrow morning."

Rory stands and shakes her head. "I need to pack. I'll see you in the morning, though, okay?"

"Sure thing, my queen."

An Unexpected Guest

Morgan

Moving goes well. I sleep most of the drive to Rory's place in the backseat of my car. Rory gets in good with Silas, Bailey, and Kit when we show up at her apartment and she's bought donuts.

Which is good, because I have something to show her. She's gonna hate it.

I can't wait.

While we're munching on donuts, I pull out the folded-up newspaper from my pocket. "Look what was published in the newspaper this week."

My friends smirk, because they already know. Rory grabs it and her eyes widen when she sees the picture. "What the—"

Now, I knew this was coming. Mrs. Patterson recruited my help, and if I may say so, I picked the perfect picture of myself to go alongside the photo of Rory in a white dress. In the photo printed next to it, I'm in a suit, a bow tie under my chin, and a canine missing from my toothy grin.

Also, we're children.

Rory hasn't said anything, but her eyes scan the article. Finally, she drops her hand and the paper crinkles in her grip.

"An engagement announcement? Really?"

"That's the one my mom clipped," Kit tells her. "You can keep it."

"I'm thinking of framing a few," I add. "Since I have so many of them."

"No," Rory says. "No way."

"Yes way." I grin at her. "People have been dropping them off at the bar ever since the announcement came out. They love the pictures of us as kids."

"It makes us look like we're child brides, or whatever the non-gendered equivalent is. Wait, how did Grandma get your picture?"

"She asked me. Actually, she asked me for a photo of us together, which"—I almost say that I obviously don't have one, but my friends might think that was pretty weird. Bailey and Silas exchange bemused glances. If they've guessed this is all fake, they haven't said anything—"I didn't think you'd want that."

"Right."

Rory picks the article up again and stares at it. Silas changes the subject. "Hey, you won't believe who Hunter added to the Save Sirens Valley Lodge group chat."

"You have a group chat?" I ask.

"Yeah. Those of us who are in, which up until last night was just Hunter and us." Silas gestures between himself and Bailey.

"In for what?" Rory asks.

The four of us exchange glances. It's not like it's a secret, exactly, but we're not talking about it just yet. Hunter, rightly so, doesn't want the rumor mill to get ahold of the idea that we might buy the lodge, and thus get all the Herevians' hopes up.

But Rory is my "fiancée." I would definitely tell her if this relationship was real.

I dust some powdered sugar off my hands. "In to buy the ski lodge."

"Save the town," Kit adds, and then raises a fist like Superman flying to the rescue.

We explain Hunter's numerous ideas to Rory. Her gaze meets mine after Silas tells her how much the lodge is listed for. "Are you in?"

I shrug. "I don't have the money."

Her mouth flattens. "This is why you wanted cash from your brother."

"It's not a big deal." I move the conversation on before Rory can put together that the ring on her finger would also be my ticket to buying in. "Who joined the group chat?"

Silas smirks. "Zachary Lawson."

My eyebrows shoot up and Kit's jaw drops. "No shit."

"Who's Zachary Lawson?" Rory asks.

"A guy we went to school with," Silas explains. "Real quiet. Comes into town sometimes, but mostly keeps to himself."

"He lives out in the woods," Kit adds. "Kind of a homesteader."

"But apparently," Bailey says, "a homesteader with enough money to buy in. Hunter said Zach just texted him out of the blue. Lord only knows how Zach even heard about it."

Huh. Zach is definitely a rugged individual who doesn't

seem to care much for local happenings—social or otherwise. "Maybe this is him coming out of his shell. Kit, we could get *him* to be our mountain man."

Kit laughs and sets his empty mug on the counter. We get to work, chuckling and trying to picture the beast of a man cleaning shirtless.

Rory's apartment is a one-bedroom, and she's selectively chosen what to pack up and what to leave behind.

"You want to bring the coffee machine?" I ask. "Even though I already have one?"

Rory looks from me to her coffee machine and back, raising an eyebrow.

"You bought a coffee machine?" Silas asks. He peers over Rory's shoulder. "Oh, that's a good one. Probably better than whatever Morgan has."

Rory smirks. I shrug and take the coffee maker out to the car.

"I better leave to pick up Grandma," Rory says, putting a framed picture on the bookshelf in my living room. She unpacked most of her things yesterday and was asleep when I got home. This morning before she sat down to work, she asked if she could make space for some items in the common rooms—even though we already said we'd make it look like she lived here, I think Rory's uncomfortable with the imposition.

Then she set up her laptop on my kitchen table and put in a full day's work.

When she called it quits, Rory paced around the house with nervous energy, moving things around and repacking items we don't have room for. Princess followed her everywhere, her tail wagging and her nose inspecting every new thing. Now she's run out of time and will have to leave things the way they are.

"Is there anything left you need me to do while you're gone?" I ask.

She shakes her head. "Just the food." I'm cooking tonight, a stir-fry Rory approved as a good first meal to serve Mrs. Patterson.

"Deal," I say. Everything's already chopped up and the rice is done on the stove. Rory disappears into her bedroom, Princess on her heels, when there's a knock on the door. Princess barks and trots to look out the front window.

Rory sticks her head out, brow wrinkled in confusion. "Are you expecting anyone?"

"No."

She watches as I stride to the door and pull it open.

Mrs. Patterson stands at my front step, with a young Black guy in a uniform who's holding a duffle bag. Between them, there's a big cardboard box that comes up to their hips and sitting on top of that is a cat carrier.

With a yowling, pissed-off Bartholomeow in it.

"Grandma." Rory comes up behind me, a warning note in her voice. "I was just on my way to pick you up."

"Good. Terrence saved you the trip." Terrence is, I assume, the young man on my porch. "Where's my room?" Rory's grandma pushes into my house, and I fall back, opening the door wider to give them space. Princess hops on her front paws, her whole body wiggling in excitement. An angry noise comes from the cat carrier.

"Princess, bed," I command.

She whines and barely even glances at me. I put more authority into my voice. "Bed."

Princess obeys, but not without looking over her

shoulder four or five times on her way to my room. I follow and close her in.

"Your room?" Rory's voice is rising as I approach. "What room? And why the hell is Bartholomeow here?"

The cat in question hisses.

"You said when the time came, you'd take Bartholomeow. Well, the time has come. I need you to take him." Mrs. Patterson wobbles on her cane into the room, and it seems like she's purposefully avoiding Rory's gaze.

"Grandma," Rory growls. "Some warning would have been nice. I didn't mean you could just drop by with the cat. Did you even think about Morgan?"

She doesn't answer.

Terrence clears his throat and leans in. "She's had to call the staff a couple times to help take care of the cat," he says quietly to Rory. "She's not supposed to spring things like this on you, but . . ."

But she's a stubborn and prideful old lady is the subtext.

Rory sighs and closes her eyes. "Grandma, you're supposed to tell me when you need help."

"It's better this way," Mrs. Patterson says, which is probably as close to an admission as she'll get. "That way I can still visit him."

Rory looks at me. She looks at her grandmother. She squeezes her eyes tight and pinches the bridge of her nose. "I'm getting a headache," she mutters.

"Uh, what's this about a room?" I ask.

Rory stands up straight and glares at her grandma.

"I'm staying the night. It'll help Bartholomeow get acclimated."

"Grandma!" Rory shouts. She flings her arms up in exasperation. "You can't just *do* things without asking!"

"Okay, okay, hold on," I say. "Let's take a few moments to calm down."

Rory grumbles but folds her arms over her chest and shifts her glare to me.

"Why don't we put Bartholomeow's stuff in the den and you can get the guest room neatened up for your grandma?" I arch an eyebrow. *And move ALL of your stuff over to my room.*

Rory sighs and stomps off. Terrence and I carry the box and the carrier into the back room. I tell Terrence I've got it from here, and he departs. Mrs. Patterson follows me, sitting on the couch and ordering me around while I unpack food bowls, toys, and a kitty litter box.

I take my sweet time unpacking and we try to coax the cat out of the carrier but he refuses to budge. That's fine, we'll have to introduce him carefully to Princess anyway.

I stand, leaving the cat carrier open. "We'll close the door and leave him alone."

Mrs. Patterson's hands are resting on her cane, her eyes on the carrier. I dust my hands off, thinking I should probably get dinner going, when she speaks.

"You can't see it right now." Her voice is small, quieter than I've ever heard her. "But he needs a good brushing. There are some mats in his fur, and . . ." Her voice trails off and she looks up at me. She doesn't say anything else for a moment, and then looks down at her hands, flexing and squeezing one of them.

"It's okay. We'll figure it out," I assure her. "There's going to be a learning curve though. I've never had a cat before."

Mrs. Patterson snorts. "They're easier than dogs. It'll take a while for him to warm up to you."

"Please," I say. "I won your granddaughter over, didn't I?"

Like You
Mean It

RORY

OF COURSE, I'M PISSED AT MY GRANDMOTHER. THE ANGRY part of me thinks she's doing this just to mess with me, to push me further to not be alone—her backup plan if Morgan doesn't work out is at least I'll have a cat.

But there's a small, niggling part of me that whispers that Grandma's getting older, frailer, and she's relieved to have me close by.

And, also, she's fucking smitten with my fake fiancé, because when they come out of the den having left the ornery cat behind, Morgan's got her chuckling. He offers us wine—he's bought some special chardonnay for Grandma, which I pass on, preferring my beer—and he entertains us while he cooks. Princess is out of the bedroom now, and she also charms my grandmother by putting her chin on Grandma's leg and insisting on pets.

It all feels so domestic. Morgan presses a kiss to the top of my head when he brings me a new beer, and when I stand at the counter to take out plates, he pulls me to him with a hand on my hip.

It's just a little hip bump, nothing too sexy or romantic about it, but Morgan sells it with his eyes, looking at me fondly, even though I'm pretty sure the angle is wrong and Grandma can't even see it.

He does this pretending thing so smoothly, whereas I just feel like cringing every time I try to offer the tiniest bit of affection. I don't know how to place my hand on his back in a way that feels natural, and when he leans in to put my plate in front of me, I tell him thanks, and then kiss his cheek. He's not expecting it, though, so I miss and get his neck instead, which is a whole different kind of embarrassing.

Before I can crawl under the table and die of mortification, Morgan sits down and lifts his glass, waiting just a beat before offering a toast. "To new families," he says.

Awkwardness forgotten, a teeny tiny lump forms in my throat as I look at Grandma. She's practically glowing with happiness.

This is why I'm doing it, right? So she can worry about me less, so she knows there's some hope of me finding love and not being alone.

"Here, here," Grandma says, and we clink our glasses. I resolve to get my shit together.

I take a sip of my beer—that IPA that I like, which Morgan has stocked in his fridge for me—and Grandma hums in appreciation for the wine Morgan chose.

She sets the glass down. "What about your family, Morgan? When will I meet them?"

I keep my eyes on my fork while I stab some of the veggies Morgan's sautéed.

"I'm not sure," he hedges.

"At the wedding?" Grandma prods. "Bridal shower? Engagement party? Don't take too long or I might die first."

"Grandma!"

Morgan sneaks a laughing glance at me. "The thing is," he says, turning back to her. "I'm not close to my mom or brother."

Grandma narrows her eyes. "Why?"

I hold my breath while Morgan thinks about it. "Rory's met my brother. He's not a good man," he says simply. "And my mother enables all of the trouble he gets into, plus she has her own problems."

Her eyes narrow even farther. "What kind of trouble?"

Morgan doesn't sugarcoat it. "Drugs. The law." He says it with a shrug, like it doesn't bother him, but I remember that hunch in his shoulders when he was on the phone with his mom and the tired defeat in his voice.

"Grandma, leave him alone."

Morgan looks up and meets my gaze. His eyes are warm and soft, but then there's a twinkle and he reaches over to smooth a hand across my shoulders. "Aw, *babe*, you don't have to protect me."

"Besides, he's going to be family soon. I want to know if he's ever been in that kind of trouble," Grandma says.

Morgan takes a bite and chews. "No, ma'am. My friends—especially my best friend, Kit, and his parents—kept me out of trouble."

"No criminal record?"

"Not even an arrest," he confirms. "Not even that time that six of us snuck into the lodge and filled the shop like a ball pit."

Grandma looks at me. "He cooks, he's got no criminal record, and he's got a lovely dog."

I throw up my hands. "One, that's a low bar, and two, I'm already marrying him, what more do you want?"

Morgan listens with amusement all through dinner as Grandma and I bicker, occasionally interrupting to defend me—or tease me—none of which Grandma fails to notice. When dinner's over, I offer to clean up while Morgan shows Grandma to her room.

I'm a bit concerned because Morgan's house doesn't have many of the accommodations that Grandma's place has, like a handrail by the toilet and a walk-in shower, but I'm not sure how much Grandma needs those things yet.

Finally, Morgan closes the door behind himself, leaving Grandma alone in the guest room. I've got suds up to my elbows as I wash the wok Morgan used—I have never even owned a wok, so I'd quickly looked up whether I could wash it regularly or if it was like a cast-iron pan—and Morgan ambles over. He rests his hip against the counter next to the sink. "She's a handful," he says fondly.

"What are we going to do?" I whisper.

"About what?" he whispers back.

"I don't know, any of it?" My voice has already risen and I check myself back to a whisper. "The cat? Sleeping arrangements for tonight?"

"The cat we'll figure out later. There's nothing we can do about that tonight. As for the second, there's only one bed left, unless you want me to sleep on the couch."

"We can't do that," I say quickly. "Grandma will probably get up in the middle of the night and what will she think if one of us is out there?"

"Well, then," he drawls. "I guess we'll just have to share the bed." The look he gives me is warm and teasing, but also carries something else that I don't want to think too much about, especially if I'm going to be sharing a bed.

Besides, it's not real.

Nerves flutter in my stomach, though they have no right to. We're cool, Morgan's a friend. And a fake fiancé. This isn't going to be weird at all. Right?

Grandma goes from her room to the bathroom and then into the den to check on the cat. Princess tries to follow her and Morgan pulls her away. Morgan and I finish the dishes and when I go to find Grandma, she's sitting up in her bed reading. She's got an iPad she uses, with the font set up so large that she swipes pages about every ten seconds, but she likes it.

"Do you want to watch something?" I ask, pointing my thumb over my shoulder to the TV.

Grandma looks at me over her glasses. "Something where the screen is too dark and the dialogue is too quiet? No."

I roll my eyes. "Fine. Morgan and I are going to watch something. Want me to close the door?"

"No," she says simply, and returns to her reading.

I'm going to close the door. Why didn't I just say that? I linger just for a moment and debate closing the door anyway, but then Princess wanders into the room and I don't want to shut her in, so I leave the door open.

Morgan's on the couch, the TV on and a slew of streaming service icons across the screen, with an arm over the back. I slump down next to him and he pulls me to him. I glance at the guest room and can just see Grandma's tablet and one hand.

Princess stands in the open doorway, watching. Her ears flick back and forth, listening while Morgan and I debate what we're going to watch, and when we settle on a sci-fi TV show neither of us has seen, she spins around and disappears, choosing Grandma.

"Traitor," Morgan huffs with a laugh. Then he slides his arm off the back of the couch and onto my shoulders, pulling me close. Butterflies take up residence in my stomach.

I shift closer, glancing at the guest room again. I fit just right under his arm, but I'm not sure where to put my hand. It hovers for a moment and then drops awkwardly into my lap.

Morgan picks it up and gives a gentle tug, using it to pull me closer. Then he drops his mouth to my ear. "Come on, my queen. Cuddle me like you mean it."

Sex Noises

Morgan

Rory is stiff as a board next to me. My arm is along her shoulders and I can feel the tightness in her muscles.

And are you surprised that this makes me want to mess with her?

Of course not.

I've still got her hand in mine, and I set them both in my lap. I tap along to the theme song of the TV show, messing up a few times because I've never heard it before. We picked a sci-fi comedy, and a few minutes in I'm laughing at the dry humor.

Rory barely cracks a smile.

"Oh come on, that was funny," I say. I shake her hand, wriggling her whole arm.

"I didn't say it wasn't."

We watch as the main character saves people from a giant alien and then reveals himself to be Alexander Skarsgård.

I poke her side. "He's not hotter than me, right?"

Rory rolls her eyes. "Do you always talk while watching something?"

"Yes," I deadpan. "Princess loves it. We share the same opinions about almost everything but she thinks *Squid Game 2* is better than the original."

Rory shakes her head, but against me, she relaxes a bit. I keep up my commentary until Rory bites her lip and turns away, hiding her laughter.

When the episode is over, Rory's sagged against me. We watch another, until I catch her covering her mouth and yawning twice during a high-action scene.

At the end of the episode, I click the TV off. "Time to hit the hay."

And just like that, Rory tightens up again.

Her grandmother comes out to say good night and Princess retreats to her bed while Rory and I take turns in the bathroom, passing each other carefully with Rory avoiding eye contact. When I emerge, clean and wearing a T-shirt and boxers, Rory's curled up on the far side of the bed, scrolling on her phone.

Without looking up, she says, "That's your side, right?"

I flop onto the bed, making her bounce. "Yup."

Her shoulders are up around her ears and she's curled in on herself. My little prickly hedgehog.

I turn off the light and pull the covers up. I stare up at the ceiling and realize I'm not tired at all. I'm on a night owl schedule, while Rory probably has to be up early in the morning. As if proving my point, Rory turns her phone off and shifts onto her back.

The wind has picked up, and I spend a few minutes listening to the rustling of the trees outside and Princess's light snoring.

When I glance over at Rory, she's awake too, staring at the ceiling. I liked the closeness on the couch, feeling her relax under my arm. We're back to square one now, though, so I'm going to have to start all over.

I shift to lie on my side. "Truth or dare?"

Rory blinks in surprise and looks at me. "What?"

"Truth or dare," I repeat. "Come on, it's been a long time since I've had a sleepover with a friend. So let's play a game."

She sighs, but even in the low light coming from the window I can see the twitch of her lips. "Dare."

"Hot damn. Let's do this right. Okay." I sit up and rub my hands together. "Show me your best dance moves."

Rory lies there for a moment, and then rolls off the bed. I reach over and turn my bedside lamp on and shove back to sit against the headboard. Princess raises her head from the bed in the corner, and then huffs and rolls onto her side, ignoring us.

On her feet, Rory shakes her shoulders out, and then takes a deep breath. First she shimmies her shoulder, then her arms swing up and over her head. Then her fists pump, her hands fly, she twirls and struts, all while she's completely deadpan.

When it hits me, I burst into laughter and she stops dancing to shush me.

"Is that the Wednesday Addams dance?" I gasp.

She flops onto her back on the bed. "Yes. I was obsessed with that show."

"Because you don't have anything in common with Wednesday Addams," I drawl.

Rory ignores my sarcasm and rolls over to prop her chin on her hands. "Truth or dare?"

"Dare," I say immediately.

"Sing a song you know all the lyrics to."

I immediately burst out into a quiet rendition of Ed Sheeran's "Shape of You." I overexaggerate crooning, putting a hand on my heart and closing my eyes.

Rory snorts. Swear to god, snorts.

By the time I finish the song, she's got her face in her pillow to muffle her laughter. I flop down next to her. "Truth or dare?"

"Truth," she says.

This one's harder to come up with, and I think for a minute. "Who was your first celebrity crush?"

"Oh no," she groans, and hides her face again in the pillow. The bed shakes, and I gasp.

"Are you *laughing*?"

"No."

She totally is. There's that laugh I've always wanted out of her. Too bad I can't see her face, but I bask in the sound until it dies out and she's just stalling. I poke her sides until I hear a muffled "Nick Jonas."

I gasp and clutch my chest. "But . . . but . . . I look nothing like him."

Rory extends a middle finger in my direction.

We play like this for a while, Rory muffling her laughter in the pillow, in the half-light of the bedside lamp and the dark recesses of the room. By unspoken rule, we alternate truths and dares.

Rory flashes the dead quiet street outside the window, and that little bit of side-boob I see gets my heart racing. I show her my last three Google searches and have to explain why I searched Spin Doctors lyrics (I had an ear worm and couldn't remember the chorus) and "toes smell like corn" (not mine—Princess's).

At some point, we hear Mrs. Patterson get up and use the bathroom. It's my turn, and Rory looks down at me. "Truth or dare?" she asks, even though she knows it's time for a dare.

"Dare."

A wicked smirk curls her lips. "Make sex noises."

I sputter.

"What?" Rory points at the wall shared with the bathroom right behind my headboard. "She's the one who invited herself to stay with a freshly engaged couple. She's *making* us share the room tonight. Don't you think that's deserved justice?"

"Oh my god." I flop facedown onto my pillow. "You are going to hell." It's muffled, but I'm sure she gets the point.

"Grandma and I will tag team hassling the devil himself. Come on." She bounces the bed next to me. "Do it, do it, do it."

"Fine, fine." I take a deep breath and push myself up onto my elbows. Rory can't stop giggling, and for that alone, I'll do it.

I thrust my hips, and there's a definite squeak and a thump. It's not bad—I've obviously had sex on this bed a lot, and if I was in danger of damaging the wall or the furniture I would have made adjustments—so I think this will actually work.

I thrust my hips again.

Eek-thump. Eek-thump. Eek-thump.

Rory goes quiet next to me. I close my eyes and build up a rhythm.

Eek-thump. Eek-thump. Eek-thump.

This is not what I pictured my first night with Rory in

bed with me like. I wanted to be naked. I wanted to be inside her, with my dick, or my fingers, or my tongue. I wanted her screaming my name.

I don't know what makes me open my eyes again—does Rory's breath hitch? Does she move? Or is it some imperceivable shift in the air?

Whatever it is, I look over and meet Rory's wide eyes.

We're Not Stripping

RORY

MORGAN'S THRUSTING AND HUMPING, HIS BICEPS BULGING and straining the hem of his shirt sleeve. His hair has fallen down over his forehead, his mouth parted, and his arms are braced. It hits me—so suddenly it knocks the laughter right out of me—that this view is rare. Intimate and yet not—if I were underneath him, I wouldn't see the muscles working or the way his toes are clenched against the sheets.

And when our eyes meet, everything else fades. I can't even hear the soft clunk of the bed frame hitting the wall anymore.

Morgan's gaze drops to my mouth. I'm not smiling anymore, and I bite the inside of my cheeks to keep myself from doing something stupid.

He doesn't look long, just huffs a laugh and lets his head fall between his balled-up fists.

Eer-thunk. Eer-thunk. Eer-thunk.

And then there's a different noise. A rapid *thump-thump-thump* on the wall and Grandma's voice comes through. "Knock it off, you two! I know you're faking it."

The thumps happen again and then I hear something clatter and Grandma curse. Morgan breaks first, laughing and collapsing into the bed.

I relax too, half burying my face into the pillow. Our gazes meet, Morgan's eyes sparkling.

I expected him to make this game sexual first, and yet I was the one who broke. I hold my breath, wondering what the next step will be.

"Truth or dare?"

"Truth," I whisper.

Morgan doesn't even blink. "What happened to your parents?"

Perhaps it's because I was expecting something to ramp up the tension inside me, so the question—invasive, personal, and serious—actually makes me relax instead of tense up.

"We were in the car," I say. "It was late. I was asleep. And we were hit by a drunk driver. I have a scar up here." I reach up to my scalp and finger the slight bare line, the raised skin. "But I was on the passenger side. My dad was driving; he died on impact. My mom and little brother died in the hospital later."

He hums and waits.

"The other guy survived. I was ten years old and—this might surprise you—I didn't know my grandmother that well. She and my mom didn't get along, and then she was my only family. Despite the distance, she came right away and sat with me in the hospital for three weeks. She was a force of nature with the doctors and lawyers, and I was just a scared kid." I can feel the pressure gathering behind my eyes, so I roll onto my back, and Morgan takes it as The End.

"You're lucky to have her," he says.

I scoff. "Sometimes."

He chuckles.

My turn. "What is your job? The other one."

Morgan props his head up on his hand to see me better. "Kit has a cleaning service—two actually. One of them is the regular stuff—cleaning rentals in the area—the other is more of a party service. Two or three of us come to the house and clean shirtless."

The side of my lip quirks up. "Didn't I say you were a stripper?"

"We're not stripping!" His protest is filled with laughter. "We have themes. Cowboys, firemen, bow ties . . . we're very popular," he says with mock modesty. "You have no idea how many bachelor and bachelorette parties we get, especially coming from the city." He shrugs. "It's all a good time." He tips his chin up. "Tell me about the last person you dated."

Apparently we're not even pretending to play the game anymore—or maybe both of us want to pull truths out of each other.

My heart rate picks up, not only because I have to think about my ex, who I realize, looking back, was pretty awful to me. I stare up at the ceiling. "We met on Hinge. She was a hairstylist, we dated for eight months. Not that long, I guess."

Morgan doesn't say anything until I look over at him. If he has any reaction to me having dated a woman, I can't tell.

"Eight months tops any relationship I've ever had." He grins at me.

I roll my eyes. "I'm not even a Herevian and I know that."

He shrugs. "I'm a bartender. In the ski season I meet a lot of women who are just passing through. And the locals —well, I've known everyone my whole life. And none of the women here have been The One. Why did you break up?"

I turn on my side to face him. Morgan lowers his head to the pillow and we both curl in. "I realized she was mean." Morgan's smile drops. "I know it's ironic, because *I'm* mean. Maybe I can dish it out but I can't take it myself."

"I don't think you're mean," he says. "Blunt, and you have a dry sense of humor. But I don't think you've ever said anything mean to me."

Probably because even I can't kick a puppy. "Tell me about your tattoos."

He sits up. "You just want to get me shirtless." Morgan's words are muffled as he strips off his shirt.

"I said *tell me about them*, not *show me them*." My words lack any real heat to them because when I catch a view of his abs, my stomach does a little flip-flop. Maybe my voice hitches too, because Morgan chuckles.

"It's a visual topic," he says. He sits up, turning away from me, and points over his shoulder at the zigzagging line on his back. It's almost like a lightning bolt, the curves softened, and there's a series of small black diamonds along the path, which disappears into a minimalist moun-tain peak. "This is Fatal Attraction, the run at Sirens that we were on when we rescued that skier. Kit, Hunter, Silas, and I all have some homage to the lodge on our bodies." He turns back to me, showing me the wings that spread over his pecs. "This is also for the lodge." He raises an arm and points at the snake. "This one I got for my mom."

My brows draw together. "I thought . . ." I don't know how to finish that. That they didn't get along? Or that she wasn't a big part of his life? Is the tattoo a reminder of good things or bad?

"I got it to remember to watch my back with her. And this quote too." He points to the grass, where the stalks form the words "O, that way madness lies."

"Shakespeare?"

"*King Lear*," he confirms. "To remind me not to dwell on what I cannot have."

"A mother?" I guess.

Morgan lies back down facing me. "Maternal love. She's always favored my brother. Always. He could do no wrong in her eyes. I think it's because our dad left while she was pregnant with me." He's quiet for a moment. "One of my first memories was of being left home alone when I was four. They went to an amusement park without me. One of my teachers called social services once because I wasn't bathing. That wasn't the last time." His voice has taken on a tone, half begging, half defensive, as if he's not sure I'll believe him.

"I believe you," I say.

He sighs and shifts to his back. "Sorry. I don't talk about it a lot. And I hate that I feel like I have to give you examples . . . like, *prove* it to you."

"I get that. I felt the same way with my sexuality, when I was dating men and just starting to realize I was interested in women too. It's hard to tell the world something without evidence. I overcompensated and talked *way* too much about my crush on Shakira for a while. How did you get through it? Therapy?"

"Are you saying I'm well-adjusted now?" There's a hint of a tease back in his voice. "I did some therapy later, but mostly it was my friends that got me through. As I got older I practically lived at either Kit's or Hunter's houses."

"You charmed your way into new families."

He gives me a sly glance. "Like yours, my queen."

I ignore that and ask him about another tattoo, since he's not done explaining them all. He shows me the pine forest half-sleeve on his shoulder, a *Legend of Zelda* tattoo on his thigh that he got as a bet when he was eighteen.

He does not put his shirt back on.

We keep talking, our voices getting quieter. At some point, Morgan turns the bedside light back off. We whisper.

The last thing I remember is the brush of a finger against my cheek and a whispered "Good night, my queen."

I WAKE UP AND EVERYTHING IS WARM. HOT, EVEN. I MIGHT be sweating. And I'm *definitely* not alone.

I open my eyes and blink them into focus. I can just make out the treetops on his shoulder.

The comforter is tucked right up under my chin, and I can see the edge of the bed and the nightstand. I've migrated across the bed. I'm not just on Morgan's side; I'm draped over him. Belly, hips, thighs, all pressed together, my toes—the traitors—are even curled under the muscles of his calf.

I knew this would happen—plenty of past lovers have complained about my heat-seeking, ice-cold toes.

His breath is slow and steady, our bodies rising and falling together, and my throat catches when I realize we're breathing in sync.

My head bounces on his huff of laughter. "I can feel you blinking, you know."

I roll off in an instant, mortified that I've invaded his space so egregiously. God, what is wrong with me? Morgan probably thinks I'm starved for attention or something. Secretly a cuddler. I'm *not.*

My roll takes me all the way off the bed. I plant my feet on the floor and grab the first thing I see that even remotely resembles pants and tug them on. Princess stands in her bed and stretches, giving a great big yawn before padding over to wag her tail at me.

The blinds are drawn and there's a soft gray light coming through the cracks. "It's early," I say. Even for me. "Go back to sleep."

"Rory—" Morgan's interrupted by the toilet flushing.

The perfect excuse. "Grandma's up. I'm going to check on her."

I step out the door and shut it behind me. I listen to Grandma wash her hands and then that door creaks open and she jumps.

"Rory, holy mother—you scared me."

"Sorry," I say. Grandma's dressed already, soft wine-colored pants and a white T-shirt. "I heard you. Want to get some breakfast?"

To my surprise, the door behind me opens. "I was thinking we could go to the coffee shop in town. It's just a few blocks over, if we want to walk," Morgan says. He's dressed in jeans and a long-sleeve shirt now, the waffly kind. It's a burnt orange that brings out the blue in his eyes.

"I can walk a few blocks," Grandma says.

We walk to Main Street, Princess on her leash making four of us, and sit outside. The coffee shop is cute and busy for a Tuesday morning. Grandma's hyper-critical of everything, as usual, but she hums in pleasure when she bites into the cinnamon roll.

Morgan knows everyone in the shop. He introduces me —"This is my fiancée"—and Grandma. He's charming, making everyone laugh, and I can't help but think of his childhood. He didn't get love and attention at home, but by charming all the Herevians, he found a new family.

When we get home, I have to get to work. Since I took yesterday off I have to catch up on my emails and billing, but it's not exactly the best environment for this, because Grandma and Morgan are trying to coax Bartholomeow out of hiding.

I'm facing the back of the house, and the door is open enough that I can see Morgan and Grandma moving around. Princess is shut in Morgan's room, so there's whining. There's also the soft crooning of Morgan's voice, the matter-of-fact statements from Grandma—"He'll be the one feeding you now, you better not bite that hand." At some point, they open a can of the good stuff and the place reeks of cat food.

Morgan is a saint to be putting up with my grandma and her ornery cat.

Eventually, Grandma wants to go home and Morgan has errands to run. He offers to drive her and she pats my shoulder and tells me not to work too hard, and she'll see me on Sunday. I'll be back from a job in Vermont by then and we have an appointment scheduled.

When they leave the house is quiet and I get way more productive . . . until I spy a cautious black head peek around the corner.

I ignore the cat—that's how he likes it.

About half an hour later, something rubs against my leg. "Hey, buddy."

"Meow."

He jumps up onto the chair next to me and then the table. He sits, tail flicking, as he surveys his new—albeit temporary—home.

I sigh. When the six months are up, and Grandma wants to move again, I'm going to have to figure out what to do about him. About everything.

I am not looking forward to it.

Pink Toe Flowers

Morgan

It's Monday, and Rory's been "living" with me for a week—in reality, she's been on a job in Vermont and then came back on Thursday for a half day of paperwork before she carried on to New Jersey all day Friday. I've been tiptoeing when I come home from the bar at night, so I don't wake her up when she's sleeping in the guest room. Any time this weekend that I wasn't at the bar, I've been working for Kit.

Like today, when Kit and I have an unusual back-to-back day. We've been busy all week—including the job I signed the NDA for.

It's the leaves. They give us a burst of activity when they're at their peak—or close to it, like they are today—and remind us that the ski season is coming up and it's time to get ready.

And that's why I'm dancing and lip-synching to Haiden Henderson while seven rowdy thirty-something women from the city howl around me. It's nearly five o'clock, and this is the last job of the day. The women are having a bachelorette party and are celebrating *hard*—but so far respectfully.

My phone buzzes on the counter, where it's close enough for me to DJ through the Bluetooth speaker, and I check the ID. My mom.

I hit ignore with a slightly soapy finger.

It buzzes again and again and again, so it's a good thing I've got it on silent, so that the calls don't interrupt the music. I ignore it in favor of singing along to the *very* raunchy song.

Kit's in the living room, I'm in the kitchen. Dish duty, while wearing a bow tie and black slacks.

Hawt.

My phone goes quiet, and I make it through about half the dishes before it starts up again. This time, it's my brother.

I *definitely* hit ignore.

It does not buzz again until I'm almost done with the kitchen. There's charcuterie fixings spread all over the counter and that makes me think we could do a chef-themed offering. Like, surely someone could put on a chef's hat and an apron while assembling appetizers and cleaning the kitchen, right?

I sigh and plan to ignore it until I see Rory's name flashing on the screen.

Shit.

I dry my hands and walk over to Kit, who's sweeping the hardwood floors. I lean into him. "Hey, can I borrow your phone?"

He grabs it out of his back pocket, unlocks it, and gives

me a quizzical look. I shrug and step out the back door, quickly finding Rory's number saved in his contacts—we made a group chat for moving her into my place—and dial.

"Kit?" Rory asks. I can hear Princess barking in the background.

"It's me," I say. "Is everything okay?"

"Your brother's here."

"Shit." I run a hand through my hair. "In the house?"

"No, I didn't answer the door. I'm sure he can see my bike out front, so he knows I'm home."

"Don't let him in," I say. This worries me. It's unlike my brother to come see me, and with the missed calls on my phone . . .

Rory snorts. "Definitely not letting him in."

"Do you need me to come home?"

Rory's quiet for a minute, thinking. Finally, she says, "He's bound to give up eventually."

"Possibly. I have like fifteen minutes left of work here, and I rode with Kit. If my brother's not gone in ten, call the police, okay?"

"Okay."

"All right, I'll be home ASAP. Thanks for calling me."

"Of course."

We hang up and I walk back into the house, throwing the door open dramatically and smoldering at the crowd of women.

They cheer, but it barely drowns out the sense of dread in my stomach.

KIT DROPS ME OFF AT HOME. RORY HAD TEXTED ABOUT eight minutes after our call to say that Graham had wandered around the property, peering into windows on the house and the garage before leaving.

When I walk in, Princess greets me exuberantly, and Rory gives me a chin dip. She recounts the whole story to me, and I tell her about the phone calls from my mom and brother. So far, I haven't responded, and the texts got increasingly aggressive, claiming I need to give the car back and that I've "stolen" it from my brother.

I stopped reading them.

"I guess they found out about the car," I remark.

Rory shrugs. "What are they gonna do? You bought it fair and square."

I snort. "Steal the car back. It was smart to make it undriveable." Last I checked, Rory had done a bit of work on the car, but not much. She'd brought a few tools from her apartment and the car was currently jacked up and the two front tires were removed, in addition to all the work she'd done when we'd first brought it home. "It'll take a lot more than breaking in and hot-wiring the car to get it out of there."

"Are you gonna call them back?"

I look off to the side, thinking. Mom was harsh enough the last time we talked, complaining that I even dared to collect the money from my brother. *How could you? He's your family.*

Skin touches skin, and I look down. Rory's reached out to pull my hand away from my ribs, where I've been unconsciously rubbing my tattoo.

The snake.

"No," I say, my voice rough. "I'm not going to call them back."

Rory nods, decisively. "Wanna order pizza and watch a movie?"

I don't know if she's trying to cheer me up or if she's just diverting the conversation, but it works. "Hell yeah."

Forty-five minutes later we've argued about and compromised on a movie, and I've picked up a pizza from Parthenope's Pies. We eat while we watch the action-packed flick, and when there's only a few slices of pizza left, Rory pushes her plate away and reclines, her head on the arm of the couch, and invites Princess to come up. My dog settles into her spot between Rory and the back of the couch, and Rory stretches out, her socked feet coming to rest on my thighs.

This is pretty great. Coming home from work, having a quiet night with the woman of my dreams—even if she is only my fake fiancée—and the best dog ever.

I rest my hands on Rory's feet and then start to rub. She hums in appreciation and I get more into it, digging my thumbs into the arches of her feet and gently pulling at her toes, a soft tease.

After a few minutes, I look up at Rory, and she's got her eyes closed instead of watching the TV. Her hair, which is down, has some chunks draped over the arm of the couch. Others cover Princess's head and fly up with each exhale from my dog's nose.

I pinch the tip of her left sock and then tug. It's a crew style, so it comes off quickly and I'm left staring in surprise and pleasure.

"What are you—" Rory interrupts herself, jacking up and trying to withdraw her foot from me. Princess barks and hops off the couch behind Rory's back, tail wagging and body starting to wiggle.

"No, no, no," I say, tightening my hold on her foot. "What is this? Are these . . . *flowers*?"

Rory squirms, and I turn my body, blocking her hands from pushing me away. Princess chuffs more, bouncing on her paws, thinking it's playtime.

"They *are* flowers. Your big toes have flowers on them."

"Morgan!"

I laugh. "They're even pink. How have you been hiding these from me?"

"Let go!" She gasps, but she's starting to laugh too. Her hands are still pushing at me though, so I lean into it, fighting against her until she gives up, her arms going from stiff to loose, and the lack of force against me causes my body to fall onto her.

I let go of her foot and catch myself on the couch, holding myself up over her. Rory's smiling, her eyes twinkling with laughter, and I love the way she looks when she's playing with me. I glance at her lips, thinking about how I would *really* like to kiss her now, if she'd let me.

But she doesn't. The laughter gets snuffed out, her lips compress together, her smile disappearing, and I inwardly sigh and push myself away.

Suddenly the space is too small. I just can't do it anymore. I can't sit back down as if nothing's happened, as if we're just roommates or pretending.

I'm not pretending.

I've never been.

I stand and Princess looks up at me, giving me an excuse.

"I'm going to take Princess for a walk," I say, walking to the door and grabbing her leash.

Rory's quiet, still lying on the couch, while I clip it to Princess's collar. Then she abruptly stands. "Why do you do that?" she demands.

I straighten and look at her. "Do what?"

Rory stalks toward me, fists clenched at her side. She

stops just short of us, between me and the door, and Princess lets out a whine.

I wait a few moments, Rory's eyes on the floor, darting around to gather her thoughts. Just when I'm about to give up, she says, "Sometimes, I swear you want to kiss me. Like maybe this isn't . . ." She hesitates, and I hear the echo of my thoughts and wonder if she thinks the same thing. "But you never do."

"Rory." I drop the leash on the floor with a soft thud. "Every time I even *think* about kissing you, you clam up. You look away, you close up, slam the shutters, raise up the drawbridge."

Rory's eyes meet mine. "I do?"

"Yeah, you do." I say it softly, hopeful that by dragging this out into the open, maybe we'll finally get somewhere.

Rory's lips bulge as she runs her tongue over her teeth. Princess snuffles and walks around us, her nails clacking on the floor.

"I have big teeth," Rory blurts.

"What?"

She repeats herself, slowly, and I can hear the edge of defensiveness that hides her insecurities. "I. Have. Big. Teeth."

This leaves me stunned. Like, yeah, she does have kind of big teeth, but her beauty is in the whole package—her narrow face, her dark hair, her stubborn chin, they all blend together to make her beautiful.

"Who told you that?"

Rory rolls her eyes and then ticks off her fingers. "Kids in school called me horse-face, once my dentist asked if I wanted to do anything about them, and my ex-girlfriend told me I would be prettier if I smiled less. And like . . ." She holds her hands out to the side. "People are always looking at my teeth. They are big. I know it. You don't have to try to sugarcoat it."

I stare at her until she looks away, and then I raise my hands to her face. "Lemme see."

"What? No." She takes a step back, hitting the door behind her.

"Come on, Rory. Let me take a look."

"Argh. Fine." She crosses her arms over her chest and looks at the ceiling. I cup her face with my hands and use my thumbs to lift her top lip up. I look around, muttering as I go. "Uh-huh, uh-huh, uh-huh. Okay. Well. Hmm."

When I feel like I've made my point, I drop my hands. I'm standing just a few inches away from her, and now that I know she *wants* to kiss me—now that she's shared this insecurity with me—nothing is going to stop me.

I wait until she's looking right at me again to say, "Still fucking gorgeous to me."

Rory huffs. "That was like the unsexiest thing that ever happened to me."

"Oh really? Do you want proof of how sexy I think that was?"

Her eyes are round, showing whites all the way around. She nods.

I grab her hand and bring it to my fly, where my dick is hard beneath the denim of my jeans. Rory's eyes widen and her hand curves, almost involuntarily around the bulge. "It wasn't unsexy to me," I growl.

Rory's gaze meets mine, and I step in closer. Her grip tightens now, her lips falling softly open. I bring my face right down to hers and whisper, "Rory Fucking Fox. You better goddamn kiss me."

Raining Sex Toys

RORY

I kiss him.

I tilt my head up and meet his lips and the moment they touch, a happy hum reverberates through Morgan's chest and into mine. His hands return to my face, gently tracing my features with his thumb while our lips play softly together.

Underneath my palm, Morgan's rock hard. The moment he placed my hand there I felt like I lit on fire. The one-eighty from his inspection of my teeth gave me whiplash, but the best kind.

I slide my hand up to his waistband and tug. Morgan closes the tiny space between us and leans into me, his mouth firmly against mine, his kiss getting harder as his erection presses into me. My back hits the door and I tilt my hips to meet his.

He moves, running kisses down my jaw to the pulse point under my ear, and I sigh and shift against him. My fingers graze the edge of his jeans to the back where I can pull him closer—as if we could get closer—and I barely notice when somewhere nearby a car door slams shut.

"Morgan—"

His mouth is on mine again, this time it's forceful and he's asking me to let him in and I do. Morgan gives me these sweeping, open kisses, our tongues just barely teasing each other with every dip, and my heart's beating so loudly I think I can hear it in my ears instead of inside my chest.

Wait, those are footsteps.

The moment I realize it there's a crash on the other side of the door. I feel it in my bones in an instant, and then I'm pulled away, Morgan spinning me to put his body between mine and the door. Princess barks madly and rushes to the front window, growling.

This time I don't mistake the footsteps running away for my own heartbeat, and Morgan throws the door open.

"Pervert!" someone shouts, and then a truck—big, black, and shiny—peels away from the curb.

We both watch Morgan's brother drive down the street.

"What the fuck?" Morgan shouts as the truck squeals around the corner.

He stands amid a mess, the porch littered with gleaming plastic and bulky shapes. The porch light isn't on, so I retreat into the house and flip the switch.

"What the *actual fuck?*" Morgan says again, this time looking down. I follow his gaze.

There are sex toys on the porch. *Lots* of sex toys. They are all in plastic packages, and there's all kinds of them. I spy a Rabbit, a butt plug, the glint of metal nipple clamps . . .

Morgan starts laughing with an edge of hysteria and

bewilderment. "What the fuck?" he repeats. "It rained sex toys on my porch."

There's also a large cardboard box slumped on its side against the front of the house. I step carefully over to it and pick it up. The bottom's busted out, and the packing tape at the top has been sliced open.

There's a label with Morgan's address on it, written out to Morgan Law and Rory Fox.

"Someone mailed us this."

Morgan turns and runs a hand through his hair. "Seriously?" He takes a step toward me and leans down to read the address. He looks back down at the X-rated debris around us. "Who is it from?"

The only return address is the local UPS store, and I turn the cardboard around looking for clues. On the side of the box is a brand name that I recognize. Even if I didn't, the sketch of the coffee machine on the side would give it away.

"This box," I say, holding the drawing up to him. "This is from a very expensive coffee machine."

"More expensive than the five dollars I paid for the coffee machine I bought you?" His lips curl into a half smile.

"More expensive than the five-hundred-dollar coffee machine I bought myself."

Morgan's eyebrows shoot up.

"This is a fifteen-hundred-dollar espresso machine. Someone has expensive taste."

"Expensive taste in coffee," he says, looking around again. "And a lewd mind. Let's gather this stuff up."

I fix the box as best I can and hold the bottom while Morgan scoops up the toys and deposits them back inside. Once we're done, he opens the door for me. "Let's take it in the kitchen."

Princess bounds up to me, sniffing loudly at the box. Morgan picks up his phone off the coffee table and types something in before following me.

I set the box on the counter and we peer in together. Each toy is still in its plastic packaging; sometimes there's even price tags.

"This is . . . quite the collection," he says. Our gazes meet and we both burst into laughter.

"What are we going to do with all this?"

"I have a few ideas."

The memory of the kiss comes roaring back to me, and I flush.

We both start pulling out the sex toys. "Some of these are clearly meant for you," he says, putting the Rabbit on the counter. "And some of these are meant for me." He pulls out a cock ring, which starts a pile on the opposite side of the counter.

When we're about halfway through, Morgan asks me, "Which one is your favorite?"

Some of these I haven't used, but there is one that I've always wanted—one that has a small cup that sucks while it vibrates. I pick it up.

Morgan plucks it out of my hand. "Good, that's definitely a keeper."

The fucker puts it in *his* pile, and now I have to try to push images of us using it together out of my mind. He smirks at me like he knows exactly what I'm thinking, but then he straightens and plucks his phone out of his back pocket. He taps the screen, his face shifting to friendliness. "Hello."

I hear Kit's voice. "What's this about a box of sex toys?"

Morgan laughs and sets the phone against the wall, so it's propped up. I lean into the camera and wave just in time to see another caller join—Bailey and Silas appear together.

For a few minutes, there's a flurry of people joining the call, some of whom I don't know—and a lot of exclamations of "what the fuck?" as Morgan retells the story several times. "My brother must have stolen it off my porch, thinking it was a fancy coffee machine. I guess he wasn't interested in the resale value of enough toys to stock a generous nightstand," Morgan jokes. "Did one of you do this? As a prank?"

"No, but I wish I'd thought of it," Kit says.

"Maybe you should call the police," Hunter adds. It's not a bad idea—if Graham stole in a moment of opportunity, what will he do when he has time to plan?

Silas clears his throat. "We got one too. Kind of."

"WHAT?" several people shout at once. Then it's kinda mayhem while people talk over each other until everyone shuts up enough to let Silas explain.

"It wasn't a big box like this," he says. "It was just one . . . uh . . . toy."

Hunter groans. "I did not need to know this."

"There was a note," Bailey adds.

I'm picking through the rest of what's in the box when I notice a white corner underneath a copy of *The Joy of Sex*. I fish it out and hold it up. It's an envelope with both our names on it.

Morgan gestures for me to open it.

"'Dear Mr. Law and soon to be Mrs. Law—or Mrs. Fox, or whichever last name you choose.'" I raise an eyebrow. "'Some generous Herevians would like to facilitate marital bliss in the bedroom. We hope you enjoy at least a few of these items and remember that open communication is the best aphrodisiac.'" I flip the card over—nothing on the back. "It's signed ex-oh."

Several voices talk over each other and Morgan raises a hand. "There's too many of us to talk at once. Best guesses, start with Kit, go!"

"Whitney Macy!" he shouts like he's on a game show.

"That's my vote too. It could be some sneaky marketing campaign," someone adds.

I have no idea who Whitney Macy is or why she would be marketing sex toys until Morgan whispers to me, "Her sex advice podcast is one of the worst-kept secrets in Here."

They take turns throwing out other names. I don't know any of them, and it starts to feel weird that I'm having a conversation about sex toys at all with complete strangers, *instigated* by even more complete strangers mailing us "marital aids." I have enough meddling with my grandmother, the rest of these nosy bodies can fuck off.

I try to swipe the suction toy from Morgan's pile and he smacks my hand away with a grin. I give up and sweep my pile into my arms and take them back to my bedroom.

I pause between the two doors. My room on the right, Morgan's on the left.

We just divided up these toys. We also just made out.

If we hadn't been interrupted, where would we be now?

I run my tongue over my teeth, a conscious move this time. Morgan says he's attracted to me, that my teeth don't bother him.

But that's what my ex-girlfriend said too. She called me hot at first. And then it was teasing little remarks. Jokes in private. Then jokes in public. Then jokes that everyone laughed at but me.

I shoulder my door open and dump the toys on the bed. They're mine, *not* ours.

On Edge

MORGAN

I CLOCK RORY LEAVING WHILE MY FRIENDS THROW OUT guesses as to who could be the Secret Santa of Smut, and I hope that's not the end of the night. I want to get back to where we were *before* my brother stole my package and threw a box of sex toys at my door. I want Rory to know that whatever flaws she thinks she has, her teeth aren't one.

Rory may be prickly and stubborn, but beneath that exterior is someone who I see is lonely. It hasn't escaped my attention that she's never once mentioned a friend, and all the pictures she's brought with her, now scattered around my house, are of her and her grandmother.

When I tap the end call button, the house goes quiet. My toys are still out on the counter so I gather them up and take them to my room, passing Rory's open door on the way. After dropping the goodies on my bed, I return to the open door.

She's lying in bed on her phone, Princess curled up behind her knees. See? My dog loves her. And everyone knows dogs are a good judge of character.

There's a suitcase on the floor, the main compartment open and clothes neatly folded up. It crosses my mind for a moment that maybe the kiss was too much, and she wants to pack her things and move out, but then I remember that it's Monday and she's probably just hitting the road in the van tomorrow. I cross my arms and lean against the doorframe. "Are you all right?"

"Fine." Her word is clipped, and then, like she thinks better of it, she drops her phone onto the comforter and shifts slightly onto her back.

I'm going to take it as an invitation.

Not a big one. But just enough.

I step forward. Princess's tail whacks against the bed and Rory's gaze follows me. I plant a hand on the headboard and reach the other down to give Princess a tiny butt scratch before I fist it on the bed.

Rory's staring up at me, eyes wide.

"I'm not quite tired yet, so I'll probably watch some TV before bed. You want to watch with me?"

She shakes her head. "I'm out of here at six tomorrow."

"All right. I'll be quiet." I smile at her and purposefully look at her mouth.

Her lips tighten, compressing in an automatic reaction to my attention. I wait a beat and watch as Rory's eyes dart around my face. Then she relaxes, starting at the curled fist I can see halfway under the pillow and ending at her lips, which soften and part for me.

I dip my head and kiss her. It's gentle and slow and I'm

not sure whose tongue moves first but then we're kissing deep and languid, our breaths matching.

The temptation to move, to put my hand to her cheek and cup her jaw and lie on top of her, gets too strong and I back away.

Rory needs time to see that I'm serious about her. She needs to see our interactions as I see them—not insincere flirting and an ingrained instinct to charm, but genuine interest in a woman I find completely, utterly fascinating.

I let my nose just barely graze hers before I whisper, "Good night, Rory," and remove myself from temptation.

I WAKE UP THE NEXT MORNING RESOLVED TO DEAL WITH MY brother and my mom. Rory's van is gone, the cat is in hiding, and the afternoon stretches in front of me before I go open the bar. Even with Princess's bubbly presence, I wish Rory were here. The floodgates are open and I want to spend all day kissing her.

Instead, after eating dinner and walking Princess, I text my brother.

GRAHAM

> Don't come to my house again or I'll call the cops.

Give me the car back and I'll leave you alone.

You stole from me.

> We bought the car fair and square. That was a good price for the work it needs. Do you have the money you owe me?

> How much is that car worth to you? Think about that real hard.

I shake my head and switch to the texts from my mom. Yesterday they started with "give your car back to your brother" and ended with "You've always held your brother back."

My finger hovers over the call button. I wish Rory were here and I'd have another distraction.

I tap it.

My mom answers on the third ring. "What have you done?" she cries. "How could you do this to Graham?"

She goes off on a tirade and I can't get a word in edgewise. The short version: my brother works so hard (untrue) and he wants to pay me back (also untrue) but it's not his fault that the dispensary got shut down (it is) and if I could just cut him some slack (because two years isn't enough) and it's not like I need the money since I'm *just* working at the bar (gee, thanks).

I stick with the same story we told Graham. "I'm getting married, Mom. I need that money to pay for the wedding."

I'm guessing—based on the Herevian gossip mill—that Mom already knew about the engagement. But she doesn't bother to congratulate me or ask when she's going to meet my fiancée.

At least she's—I think—sober.

I know that I'm not going to walk away from any conversation with my mom as the good guy. But I can't stop trying.

I let her talk, trying to tune it out. *Two more minutes. I'll give myself two more minutes to try to get her to see my side of it.*

It doesn't work, and when the timer on the call clicks over to a new minute, I tell my mom I gotta go.

"I'll tell Graham to come by again," she says.

"Don't," I say, but she's hung up already.

I wait on edge in the backyard, throwing tennis balls for Princess and expecting my brother to come by at any moment. I'm glad the ring is with Rory and the car is shut up in the garage.

He doesn't come, and I go to work.

Heart Eyes Emoji

Rory

The drive to the Cape gives me a lot of time to think. I mean, I mostly think about kissing Morgan—pressed up against the door, his mouth hard and hot on mine, but I also think about the good night kiss. Soft and gentle while pulling back just enough to tease.

It's distracting for a while, but not enough to completely keep my mind off the confession prior to the kiss. The way Morgan had looked at me had almost made me not care about my smile.

I know I have big teeth. I know I'm not conventionally pretty.

But Morgan seems to find me attractive anyway. That hard-on under my hand was . . .

I shake it off. I'm driving. I need to focus and getting aroused while on a work trip is not ideal, especially because

I did not pack a vibrator—not even one from the box of smut.

I sigh. Four days on the road is going to be a long time alone with my thoughts.

When I broke up with my ex, I started seeing a therapist. In the beginning, we talked a lot about my physical insecurities, my small circle of friends (many of whom were my ex's friends and, thus, no longer mine), my inability to form friendships, and the lingering grief over my family's death. Eventually, I stopped scheduling the appointments. I was talked out, and nothing new was happening in my life anyway.

Lately, I think I've been so focused on trying to get my grandmother settled somewhere that I've forgotten I have my own life.

Morgan barreled in with the reminder that I am more than a granddaughter, more than an orphan, and more than someone who's lost a sibling (why isn't there a word for this?). After everything I've learned about him, it's only fair that I look back over every interaction with Morgan in a new light, observing him not as someone who can't help but flirt with everyone he meets, or someone that views my tough exterior as a foil to his charm, but as someone who actually might be attracted to me.

Did I think I was so undeserving of his attention and attraction? These thoughts plague me all through my drive, the meeting with the warehouse team, and running some tests on their malfunctioning articulated robot.

And that night in my hotel room, I book a therapy appointment.

I wish that I had someone else I could talk to—not a paid professional but a close friend. I'd even take talking to Grandma but what would I say to her? I'm surprised my fiancé *actually* likes me?

I also have a text from Morgan—several actually.

MORGAN

Drive safe.

Barty says hi.

What do you do for dinner when you're on the job?

That second one includes a picture of Bartholomeow loafing on the top of Morgan's fridge, looking annoyed that he has to tolerate paparazzi.

I send Morgan a selfie of me with my Thai takeout. He's probably at work right now, and I'm tired from the long day's drive, so I fall asleep before he can respond.

In the morning, his response is waiting for me, sent around 10 p.m.

MORGAN

Hello gorgeous.

He added a heart eyes emoji, and it makes me smile. A second text came at almost midnight.

MORGAN

I'm getting ready for bed, and I expect you'll be reading this when you wake up. So, good morning, my queen.

Morgan and I text all week. Sometimes it's just random photos that I respond to with emojis: Princess with four tennis balls in her mouth, upside down on the lawn; Miss Mullins's T-shirt that she wears on Wednesday with Rosie the Riveter saying "Let's take down the patriarchy"; the view down Main Street during a walk with Princess where the trees lining the road have turned bright, vibrant yellow. I respond in kind: a picture of a bandaged finger when I sliced my cuticle open on a clamshell package (he responds with a kissing emoji), a Catskill Mountains bumper sticker I spot on a Subaru, and the fall foliage here on the Cape, which isn't as vibrant as upstate yet.

Every message sends a thrill through me.

Maybe I am unused to this kind of attention. The crescendo of flattery is battering my defenses. Grandma loves me, I know that. But her love is like a thief in the night sneaking in and leaving a somewhat formal letter on your pillow that ends with "Love, Grandma," whereas Morgan's affection is like coming home to a battered front door, rose petals trailing to the bedroom and an effusive and slightly R-rated (with illustrations) love note instead.

But it's also terrifying. Every photo just furthers this idea that Morgan is so rooted in Here and I am not. Grandma and I both ignore this truth—no matter where she settles, I will still be living on the road most of the time.

Thursday morning I wake up with a different sort of text from Morgan.

MORGAN

Hey, you didn't come by the house, did you?

Never mind.

Call me when you can, no matter the time.

It's six thirty, and I dial anyway, lying on my side in the hotel bed.

"'Lo?" Morgan's voice is scratchy and sleep-laden.

"It's me."

"Hey." The automatic softening and warmth sends my heart fluttering. Even mostly asleep, Morgan's affection comes through loud and clear. "How are you?"

I can't help but smile into the phone. "You told me to call you? Remember?"

"Oh shit, yeah." He's much more alert now. "Someone broke into the garage and the house."

I sit up. "What? Is the car still there?"

"Yeah it is, but a window's broken. The glove compartment was open, and in my house any paperwork I have was ransacked."

"Oh my god." I run a hand over my face. "Your dipshit brother doesn't even know how to break into a car."

"I know. He's more of a—wait, do you know how to break into a car?"

"Of course."

"God you're hot," he says, and I laugh.

"Did you call the cops?"

"Yeah. They came by to look at things. I told them about the situation and they said he was probably looking for the paperwork."

The sigh in Morgan's voice is heavy, and in the silence I think about the stress of coming home from a late night and having to deal with all that. And even after the cops left, Morgan had to grapple with his brother violating his space.

"Are Princess and Bartholomeow okay?"

"Yeah. She was locked in my bedroom and Barty was probably hiding somewhere. They're both fine."

I pull the covers up over myself. "And you're okay?"

The concern in my voice is so embarrassingly obvious, I might as well be waving a white flag. *Look at me! I care about you!*

Morgan sighs. "Yeah."

We're both quiet for a moment, and I bite my lip. It wasn't a convincing "yeah."

"Hey. Wanna hear about the robot I'm fixing?"

There's a hint of amusement in Morgan's voice when he says "yeah" and I tell him all about my project here, his "ohs" and "uh-huhs" getting softer until he falls asleep.

Get a Room

Friday afternoon I'm in the bar. It's too early for the happy hour crowds just yet, but there are a few leaf peepers sitting out back having a drink. We have a row of Adirondack chairs lined up just outside the big picture windows with fire pits scattered about. On weekday afternoons in ski season, it'd be full of parents waiting for their kids to finish practice, but now it's for the tourists. The yawning expanse of The Enchanted Meadow, the front of the mountain where trails merge and the base of the chairlift sits, is dry grass and the trees are in full color.

The cowbell sounds and I look up to welcome the next tourist, but instead Rory saunters in. I knew she would be back today, but I didn't expect her to come here.

"Hey," I say, clearly delighted, and she returns my greeting with a crooked smile, and instead of taking her usual seat she walks down the bar. "No helmet?" I ask, clocking her empty hands. I walk along my side of the bar and meet her in the pass-through.

"No, I'm still in the van."

She didn't even go home yet. She drove right into town and came to find me first. She's still in her jeans and polo from work, her leather jacket layered on top and her hair up in a top knot—a sure sign she hasn't been riding.

I grin down at her. She tilts her chin up and before I even realize what's happening her lips are on mine.

It's a quick kiss, but hell yeah I'll take it.

She eyes the dopey smile on my face and rolls her eyes. "It's just a kiss, calm down." But she's holding back a chuckle.

I reach out and snatch her by the hips and pull her into my arms, bending her over backward while invading her mouth. Rory's surprised yelp is cut off by my lips, and it fades to a groan as we both deepen the kiss.

I sweep both arms around her and she does the same. Her shirt rides up, and my fingers graze her waist while hers tangle in my hair. I pull her closer to me, wanting her stretched against me. I've missed her all week, even if it's the norm for us.

My hand glides up her back, fingers tracing along her spine until I've rucked her shirt up so much my palms ride over the back of her opposite ribs. My other hand has gone farther south, delving into the back pocket of her jeans. This is not the tight jeans she wears on her bike, but a looser, softer fit. She smells like metal and leather and fall and—

"Hey, get a room!" Paul shouts from the kitchen. Then he dings the bell and I'm guessing the nachos are ready for the couple outside.

I break the kiss but don't pull away. My forehead goes

to hers and I wait while Rory pulls herself back together. She's breathing hard, and when her eyes open, her pupils are huge.

I'm sure mine are too.

"With you," I say, and have to clear my throat before I can continue, "it's never just a kiss."

EARLY THE NEXT MORNING—THE BAR CLOSES AT MIDNIGHT on Fridays, so I don't get home until one thirty or so—I sneak into the darkened house. After the scorching kiss in the empty bar, Rory had opted to head home, and my night got busy. Around ten, when things were starting to wind down, I finally had a breather and could look at my phone. Rory had sent me a picture of Princess and Rusty, the fourteen-year-old girl who lives next door, playing in the backyard. *I met your neighbor*, she'd said.

I don't blame Rory for not staying at the bar. It was crowded and busy and I wouldn't have been able to spare her any attention. I'm sure she was tired from her workweek and glad to be home, though I'm not sure my place feels like home yet.

I tiptoe through the den and into the kitchen, where movement and a glint catch my eye, and I jump nearly two feet off the ground.

The glint blinks at me. Oh, it's Bartholomeow.

"Hey buddy," I say. He flicks his ear and watches as I resume tiptoeing. My door is open, my room dark, which is expected. Princess is probably in there, snoozing in her bed. But when I flip on the bathroom light, Rory's door is open too.

I frown. She's obviously asleep by now, so maybe

Princess was with her and she left the door open for my dog?

I lean into the doorway and grab the knob to close it before realizing that Rory's bed is empty. My first thought is that something's wrong. Rory's van, bike, and car are all here, my driveway menagerie full. Where could Rory be?

A small, hopeful voice murmurs at me to check my bed. And there she is, an unmistakable plateau under the covers.

I bite my knuckle and fist-pump.

YESSSSSSSS!

I quickly shower and brush my teeth before crawling into my side of the bed. Princess snores gently from the floor and Rory shifts slightly. She mumbles before wriggling across the bed to curl up against me.

My face hurts—I've smiled all the way through the bedtime ritual—but I finally doze off with my queen in my arms.

Sit on Your Throne

Rory

I wake up completely wrapped up with Morgan again.

This time Morgan's still asleep. His breathing is deep and even, which makes sense because it's dark out. He didn't get in until late, whereas I've been asleep for almost eight hours.

So I let myself bask in the warmth of Morgan's embrace until nature calls too loudly to ignore anymore. I carefully slip out—Morgan grunts his displeasure, even in his sleep—and use the bathroom. Instead of cooking, I make coffee and eat a snack bar and an apple from his fruit bowl and read on the couch. Bartholomeow curls up next to me.

The sun is up in full by the time Morgan wakes. In his boxers, he shuffles to the bathroom, and the cat slinks off. I get up and let Princess out to pee and stand in the back door in my sleepwear, one hip cocked against the frame, and let her sniff around for a few minutes.

Morgan comes up behind me, the soft pad of his feet and the swishing of fabric the only warning I get before he wraps his arm around me and hauls me off my feet.

"Morgan!" I squeal and laugh while he shifts me around to drape over his shoulder. Princess barks and clambers onto the porch and then through the door. Morgan shuts it behind her and carries me through the house, his covered butt just inches from my swaying face.

Then the world flips right side up and I bounce on the bed once before Morgan smothers me. His mouth is on mine, hot and demanding. He tastes like mint, so he must have brushed his teeth, and he doesn't seem to care that I taste like coffee. His hips notch perfectly between my legs and he's already hard.

My sleep shorts are thin, and the press and grind of his erection against me makes me gasp. Morgan pulls back and smooths my hair away from my face, his eyes lidded and a cocky smile curling his lips.

I pull his head down and we're making out. My hands trace all over his body, everywhere I can reach—up his back and shoulders, feeling the muscles work as he holds himself up, his weight and pressure just right as he invades my mouth.

We kiss until I can't breathe properly, until I have to tear away from his mouth and take in big, gasping breaths. Morgan takes advantage of my turned head to work his way down the side of my neck. His kisses are light, a soft murmuring against my skin, until he nips my pulse point and my hips buck up against him of their own accord.

He traces light kisses and hot breath, alternating with teeth and tongue. His finger tugs the strap of my top down and the cold air on my exposed breast is immediately replaced by a warm hand and then a hot mouth.

Everything in me gets tighter and tighter. It's hard to focus on any one point of my body when there's so much to take in—the soft hair threaded through my fingers, the way my feet flex with every grind of his body into mine. I'm aching and can barely remember my own name, so it's a miracle that I can remember his. "Morgan."

He switches to my other breast, ignoring my plea. That's fine, I have no idea what I was going to say, what I want to ask for. I can't even *think* thanks to the sharp pinch of his teeth on my nipple.

He sucks hard once and lets go with a pop. I shudder against the bed and he rests his chin on my stomach, looking up at me.

"Rory, I want to make you come."

My eyelids flutter.

"I want you to ride my face. Would you do that for me, Rory?"

I nod, and he lurches up and rolls to the side.

"Thank fucking god." Morgan stretches out, and then points to his face. "Suffocate me."

I laugh, which only encourages him. He pats his chest. "Come on, get up here."

I sit up and shimmy off my underwear and shorts before swinging a leg over his waist. He's warm against my skin, most of my thigh and my ass resting against his boxers, but still feeling the heat anyway. Where my knees rest against his bare skin, though . . . it's scorching.

My eyes are drawn down to the snake tattoo. One coil of the snake sits right against the inside of my knee. I reach out and trail a finger over the ink. Beneath my fingertips, Morgan hums in response.

I trace it to the front, where I can follow the V-cut

down to his waistband. Morgan groans, but he likes it. He stretches his arms overhead, lacing his fingers together behind his head to allow me this interlude.

And then there's the cut up the center of his abdomen. Morgan's got to be the fittest person I've ever been with— not soft curves or gentle flesh. Harder. Tighter.

The pad of my middle finger runs up his chest. I raise up a bit, leaning forward, and trace another tattoo—the wings. I follow a feather until it ends, and keep going to his nipple.

When I run my finger over it, Morgan takes a sharp breath and I finally look up. His eyes are dark and deep, any traces of laughter gone. "Come on. Sit on your throne, my queen."

My stomach dips, this intensity from Morgan something I'm not prepared for. I roll my eyes, striving for levity. "That's cheesy, even for—"

Morgan's hands leave his head at the same moment his hips rise up from the bed and his chest bumps me. I fall forward with a squeak and Morgan catches my thighs, diving his arms between my legs and tugging me up to his mouth. I catch myself on his headboard and then I lose track of everything the second Morgan's tongue touches my pussy.

I close my eyes and leave him in charge. Fingers dig into my hips, pulling me down, down, down, as he groans into me.

Morgan traces my opening, his tongue broad and flat while his scruff abrades my inner thighs. He pulls me down harder, and I think *he really does want me to suffocate him.* But clearly he can breathe, because he goes at it with gusto. He teases me, barely paying attention to my clit, and I think it's all a ploy to torture me.

And the noises he makes! He hums and grunts and

groans in pleasure and I feel every sound in my nerves. He flicks and teases, driving me wild.

Finally, he sucks on my clit, and I gasp and curl into him. One hand leaves the headboard and grabs his head, and my thighs tighten. I'm getting close, and I can vaguely hear myself crying out, maybe even—ugh—*begging*.

And then I break.

Lost in Pleasure

MORGAN

RORY PULSES ABOVE ME, CRYING OUT AND GRINDING against my face.

I'm in heaven.

I could tell Rory was worried about putting too much of her weight on me, but toward the end, she was pressing against me, mindlessly seeking her own pleasure, and it was hot as fuck.

Plus, I could watch her. Her eyes were closed, so maybe she didn't realize I was paying attention, but her grip on the headboard, the way her lips fell open and she gritted her teeth, and the bouncing of her breasts above me was the best fucking view I've ever seen in my life.

There's nothing sexier than seeing Rory Fox lost in pleasure.

I keep working my mouth on her as long as she lets me.

She shudders and clenches and I keep sucking until she gasps and her eyes fly open. Her hand in my hair pushes my forehead away and her hips pull back, falling away and to the side. Rory collapses on the mattress, head down toward the foot of the bed, and I'm drawn back to my own body, my own needs. My cock aches and throbs and the full taste of Rory lingers in my mouth and her scent is all I can smell.

We lie there for a moment, both of us panting. I get up first, propping myself up on my elbows. Rory's curled on her side, her eyes closed and her mouth slightly parted.

I lean to my left side and place my free hand on her hip. Her eyelids flutter open and she glances at me out of the corner of her eye.

"That's a good throne."

I chuckle. "You did a really good job sitting on it." I run my hand up as far as I can reach, over her ribs and up to the small mound of her breast and give it a gentle squeeze. Her eyes close again.

"Give me another minute."

My hand stills on its path back down her body and I frown. The unspoken words are "and then it's your turn," and that won't do. Good sex is not a tit for tat, not an obligation. *I got mine so now you get yours.*

I scoot closer, pressing my stomach against her back. If she was facing the other way, my dick would be right in her face, but it's not.

I lift my head and wedge my left hand between Rory's thighs from behind to give myself some space. Her body's limp and pliable still, making it easy for me to slide my right hand over her belly and find her clit again.

She jerks. "What are you——?"

I stop. "Too sensitive?"

"A little."

"Want me to stop?"

There's a pause, and then she relaxes back down. "No."

I press against her, the pad of my fingers trapping her clit while I circle against her. With my mouth free, I press kisses on her hip and the outside of her thigh. As she starts to squirm, I rest my cheek on her and watch.

It's more subtle this time; a bitten lip, her fist gripping the comforter, and then the press of her hips forward, dislodging my headrest while she comes against my hand.

Okay, I can't take it anymore. I roll to my back, away from Rory, and take my cock in my hand, pumping an embarrassingly few times (not that she's going to notice) before I get my own release, spilling on my chest.

We lie there, both of us quiet and catching our breath. I should be exhausted—I was up late and it's still early for me—but I'm wired. I want to do that all over again now, and then every day for as long as Rory will let me.

But Rory might be asleep next to me. She's gone still and her breathing is even. I sit up, looking down at her, and contemplate sneaking out of bed. As if in agreement, my stomach rumbles, and Rory's eyelids flutter open.

I bend down and kiss the closest skin—the side of her knee. "I'll make breakfast."

Why Is He Naked?

Morgan

"You want me to ride *that*?" Rory asks.

Boing.

"Hey, she may not look like much, but she's perfectly safe," I say.

Boing.

Rory does not look convinced.

Boing.

"Everyone else is already at the top," Hunter says helpfully from the control box.

Boing.

"Kit is keeping an eye on us from there," Hunter continues, "and I'll ride up right behind you."

Boing.

"So I'm supposed to get on this metal death contraption—"

Boing.

"—with you and a hyperactive dog—"

Boing.

"—without any snow to cushion me if I fall?"

Boing.

"Princess isn't making her case well right now since she's turned into a canine pogo stick," I say. We all look at the dog in question.

Boing.

"I swear she'll be professional when we give her the go-ahead," I promise. "She's just too excited now."

"Also," Hunter says. "Don't you drive a motorcycle at seventy miles an hour pretty regularly?"

Rory glares at him. "Eighty. Fine. How do we do this?"

Once the next chairlift passes, I give Princess an "okay" and she leaps onto the upcoming bench before it even gets halfway around the bend. I get Rory into position, and when the seat hits the back of our legs, we sit.

Princess barks happily, but the chairlift swings a little as we take off and Rory grips my arms. "Hang on," I say, "let's get the bar down."

Once we've got our shoes on the footrest and the bar over our laps, Rory eases up a smidge. Or at least, she lets go of me. I put my arms on the back of the chair as we sail up into the treetops.

After orgasms and breakfast yesterday, we walked Princess before I had to go into work. Fortunately I remembered to tell her at the last minute to keep this morning open to come hang out with my friends. Sunday Funday is a once-a-month ritual we have (yes, there's even a group chat for it) where we get together and play games over brunch. The October one is particularly special because we time it with the foliage. It's early in the morn-ing, because most of us are kept busy during the day with the tourists, so that sucks, but it's worth it to spend time with my favorite people.

Which now includes Rory.

It's a warm day—no wind, plenty of sun—and the deciduous trees are full of color. Most of the trees are deep green pines on the mountain itself, but behind us, the valley stretches out, flush in yellow and gold.

It's the perfect day for Sunday Funday.

"Wow," Rory says, and my chest swells with pride as we rise up the mountain. "Is that where the ski runs are?" She points down below us where there's a wide, bare path through the trees.

"One of 'em. It's harder to see the runs when there's no snow on the ground, and there are some cuts in the trees for utilities and such. Look over there." I point out to the left, where there's a sign approaching. "Watch behind us and you'll see the trail names."

We both look over our shoulder to see the sign that declares that the winding green, Odyssey's Path, goes off to the left and the black, Fatal Attraction, heads straight down.

"And then over there," I point up above the crossing and again to the left. "There's a small sign. That's one of the hiking trails that comes through."

"Are there a lot of hikers?" Rory asks.

"Not as many as there used to be," I say. "It's peak season now though, with the fall foliage." The competition for hiking trails is tougher than for its ski runs; there are many good trails in the area for hiking, but we're closer to New York City than the other Catskills ski areas.

Rory's quiet, gazing into the trees and admiring the view. Princess pants to my right side, whining occasionally from sheer excitement. She loves coming up to the mountaintop, especially because she knows Donny, Leo's dog, will (probably) be there and she'll get to play largely unsupervised.

"Is that . . ." Rory begins, peering into the trees ahead of us.

I look out and see exactly what she's noticed. "A bra? Yup."

"Why *on earth* would someone take off a bra up here? Wait, did they do it in winter?"

"Yeah, it's a bit of a tradition. It's not as popular here as some of the bigger places, where you'll get whole trees full of bras and panties."

"Bras *and panties*?" Rory stares at me, horrified. "How exactly does one get their underwear off in the cold without falling off a chairlift? Or getting their delicate parts frostbitten?"

"Delicate parts?" I ask, dropping my voice down. "Wasn't very delicate last night."

Rory flushes and shoves me lightly. "You know what I mean."

"Huh. Well, it's definitely trickier when you've got all your layers on but let's see what I can do here." I start to unbutton my jeans.

"What? Morgan! No!"

I do a shimmy to get my pants down under my ass. Hmm. My boots are going to be a problem.

"Morgan!"

Princess barks.

"Easy, girl," I say. I quickly pull both boots off and tie them together, tossing one over the lift bar so that they dangle on either side of it.

"What the hell are you doing, Morgan?" Hunter shouts from behind us.

I hand Rory my jeans. "Mind your own business, Hunter," I shout over my shoulder. I lift one cheek and then the other, sliding my underwear down. "Whew, that seat has a crack and it pinches."

Hmm . . . the top station is getting pretty close. Not sure I'm gonna make it.

Rory's got her hands over her face, laughing too hard to say anything and peeking out at me from between her fingertips.

"Kit, Morgan's coming in hot," I hear from behind. "You might want to slow the lift a bit if you don't want a look at full-frontal Morgan."

The radio squawks and I hear Kit's response: "*Why is he naked?*"

The lift does *not* slow, a clear challenge from Kit, and I whip my underwear over my head like a lasso and then fling it out into the trees. I can see why the few bras out here are bright reds and pinks; I can barely tell where my gray boxer-briefs land.

"Jeans, please." I hold out my hand and Rory wordlessly passes me my pants.

"Hmm," I muse. "I don't think getting the pants on is going to be as easy as getting them off."

Princess barks, and I'm guessing that's because she's spotted Kit. Sure enough, when I look up, my friend lounges against the control panel, arms crossed over his chest.

Eh. There's nothing to do but protect the little bit of dignity I have left. I wad my jeans and put them in my lap to cover myself up.

The chairlift slows and comes to a stop.

"Morgan." Kit sighs, shaking his head. "What the hell are you doing?"

"I'm sorry," Rory begins. "Does anything about this"— she waves her hand to encompass my whole body—"actually surprise you?"

Kit tips his head back and laughs. "No, but I'm still gonna give him hell for it."

I ignore them and raise the bar. Princess whines until I say, "Go ahead, girl" and then she launches herself off the chair and out onto the mountaintop.

"Anyone who doesn't want to see Morgan's ass, avert your eyes!" Kit shouts.

There's a series of hoots and hollers coming from the picnic table set up to the right. I stand from the lift, socks sinking into the grass, and turn my back on the group. I grin at Hunter on the chairlift behind us while I shake out my jeans and pull them on one leg at a time. I turn around while buttoning up to find Kit and Rory both watching me.

Kit's bemused, winking at me before telling me I have a great ass, but could I please move now so he can get Hunter up here? Rory's got her arms crossed, her hip cocked, and a more appreciative eye for me.

"Just for that," she says, "next time I plan to ride the chairlift up I'll shove a bra in my pocket."

"Cheater," I say as we join my friends.

Sunday Funday goes like this: we've got a picnic table set up, one of those big round ones that'll seat ten. It's perched a few feet from the lip of The Bone Meadow, a steep and wide black diamond that has the best view of the valley from the edge. Everyone brings stuff—Hunter brought our food up on his lift so I could manage Princess and my queenly newbie without worrying about it—so the table is laden with breakfast sandwiches, fruit, burritos, juice, and even a couple bottles of bubbly for those of us who don't have to go directly to work.

I put Rory between Bailey and Kit, since she knows them the best. It also happens to be the best seat in the house. Leo and I sit with our backs to the view, keeping an eye on our dogs. It takes Donny a while to warm up to Princess no matter how many times they've played together. Either that or the lazy, placid pit bull is too bewildered by my dog's bouncing energy to engage.

Bailey, Leo, Quinn, and Rory don't have to work today, so the sparkling wine flows. Silas is at an open house, Tuan will probably have to leave early because he needs time to cook before his restaurant opens, and Jared will be leaving around the same time I do so he can open the brewery, but it's nice to have most of us together at least once a month in the off-season.

Now that I know how Rory feels about her teeth, I see it all over her interactions. The way she purses her lips to the side instead of smiling when she and Quinn talk about hot-wiring cars, the way she bites into food and carefully chews it—and also the way I get a flash of her teeth when she catches me watching her and she just can't help herself.

I want to earn her smiles all the time.

When everyone's done eating, we pack up the food and clear the table. Hunter pulls out two decks of cards. "Okay, we've got a newbie here today, so we'll do an easy round first."

"Whoa, whoa, whoa. An easy round?" Rory's brows are knitted together. "You don't even know that I'm a newbie."

"Oh, you're a newbie," Bailey says into her wine, which is rich because she only started coming to Sunday Funday when she moved here.

Hunter ignores the interruptions. "The name of the game is 'Whose Turn Is It Anyway?' and the base play is like Uno. Suits follow suits, face value follows face value, the first player to get rid of all their cards wins. All the other rules . . ." He leans forward and whispers, "are a secret."

Everyone obliges with a long "Ooooooo."

Hunter makes a big show of plucking one card out of the stack, looking at it, and putting it back. Then he reshuffles and deals out seven cards each, and the play begins. We make it twice around before Hunter interrupts game play and pulls a card from the stack for Bailey. "Penalty for playing out of turn."

Bailey groans. Rory's just played an eight, and Kit crows on her other side and plays a card. Game play resumes, in the opposite direction.

"Wait, what?" Rory asks.

"Watch and learn, my queen," I tell her.

Tuan plays the next eight, and since most of us have caught on, the play is reversed, and no penalties are handed out.

"So does that mean every time an eight is played, someone has to—"

Rory's cut off by Bailey's hand covering her mouth. "Shh, you don't want to get a penalty."

"Oof, Bailey." Hunter shakes his head and pulls a card. "Penalty for revealing a rule of the game."

"What!?" Bailey throws a hand up. "I was protecting her! Guarding the newbie!"

"Nah, seconded," I say.

"Damn you!"

Play continues, until we go a few rounds with no penalties. "Okay," Hunter says, tossing his cards into the center. "Let's play for real."

Oh, It's On

Rory

"Jared, present your trophies."

At Hunter's words, Jared reaches under the table and raises up the most god-awful trophy I've ever seen. It is, actually, a trophy, and not one of the cheap plastic ones either, but it's dinged and scuffed and it has a faded old ribbon tied to the bottom and a fake plant sticking out of the top.

Etched on the base is "Ruler of the Sirens."

"And," Jared reaches down again and this time pulls out a brown paper bag. From it he pulls out an unmarked, sealed beer bottle. "This is," he says, "four bottles of the underground Golden Voice pilsner. It'll be the best fucking thing you've ever put in your mouth . . . no offense to present company of course."

There's sputtering laughter from around the table and glances cast at me and Morgan while my cheeks heat.

"This is from Dad's own limited run, never to be sold. I'll fucking disown you if so much as a peep of this beer's existence gets out."

"Holy shit," someone murmurs.

Golden Voice is the local brewery, the same one that makes the Call of the Wild IPA that I love so much.

Morgan catches my eye across the table. His brows furrow and he purses his lips, like *I've got this.* And I know exactly what he's thinking. I'm the *newbie*, no one's expecting me to win, so Morgan's going to win those bottles for me.

Oh, it's on.

Hunter sorts out a run of cards, ace through king, laying them face up on the table. Then he flips them over, shuffles, and fans them out for us to pick. "This way," he explains, "there's only one rule per face value." I draw an ace. Whatever Morgan draws makes him chuckle, and when I raise an eyebrow at him, he flashes me a wide, dangerous smile.

Oh boy.

After everyone's picked a card, Hunter collects them all and shuffles again. "The training wheels are off; everyone gets to come up with a rule and enforce it." He's speaking for my benefit, of course.

The newbie.

"What are the hard limits?" I ask.

"Hard limits?" Hunter's hands slow.

"You know," Kit interrupts. "Water sport, blood play."

"Spanking," Morgan adds.

"Whips."

"Anal."

"Okay, okay, okay." Hunter waves his arms. "I get it,

Tweedledee and Tweedledum. However, I don't think that's quite what your fiancée means."

"Well," I start. "I'm guessing regular Uno game play is allowed—reverse, skip, draw cards."

Hunter nods. "No rules that make anyone draw more than four cards, though. We'd be here forever."

"Got it," I say.

"Light humiliation," Morgan adds.

"What?"

"One time Silas made everyone who played a certain card cluck like a chicken," Hunter tells me with a grin.

"A PG version of truth or dare." I glance at Morgan and his gaze goes soft. Memories of our game of truth or dare flash in my mind, but I force the thought away. "So what's out of bounds and what's acceptable?"

"Nothing that requires too much time or getting up from the table," Hunter says. "Other than that, someone can object and we'll deliberate."

"This isn't a fucking federal court," Jared mutters.

"Plus," Kit adds, "you have to be willing to do whatever it is yourself if you play the card."

Good point.

Hunter finishes dealing out the hand. "Everyone have their rules in mind?"

Heads around the table nod.

And Hunter flips over the top card.

THIS GAME IS *BRUTAL*. IT'S NOT A SKILL GAME. IT'S entirely a memory game, and the shit people make up is bananas.

At one point, Hunter plays a queen and Morgan

reaches for the deck. "Penalty for not genuflecting to Rory."

Hunter cackles, accepting the penalty card and then giving me a bow and twirling his hand while saying, "My queen."

My face goes beet red, and I reach across the table in Morgan's direction but he ducks out of range, shoulders shaking from laughter. The whole table is laughing, and I can't decide if I want to punch Morgan or kiss him.

"What does genufelting mean?" Leo asks, once the laughter has died down, and his mispronunciation has me biting back another chuckle.

"Genuflecting means, like, showing deference," Bailey explains. "Bowing or some such."

"Got it."

The other rules are less embarrassing. Whoever plays a seven gets to switch hands with a player of their choice—Kit's rule. On a four, the player has to sing the opening lines of "Hooked on a Feeling" by Blue Swede with the rest of us doing the backup—Tuan's rule. There's a kerfuffle when Bailey spills her drink and everyone makes a mad rush to grab a penalty card while shouting "Party foul!" There's penalties for not enforcing rules, there are penalties for playing out of turn, and there are penalties for taking too long—when no one wants to admit they can't remember whose turn it is and everyone casts glances around until someone finally doles out the penalty.

Leo gets a penalty for forgetting his own rule—a jack reverses game play—and everyone nods approvingly when they discover my rule—you have to pick a random card from the person to your left and play it.

Jared goes on a bender because he has neither a four nor a diamond and has to draw until he can play. "Fuck, fuck, fuck, fuckity, goddamn fuck, I hate you all," he seethes over their laughter, until his hand is at least twenty cards.

Tuan's the first to get down to one card but then Hunter, in a strategic move, plays a seven, so he and Tuan switch hands. But then the suit shifts to hearts and then-Tuan's-now-Hunter's card can't be played.

Several other people get to a single card and then have to draw.

But Grandma and I played Uno a lot growing up. And I have a very good memory.

And today I also have good luck.

I'm down to two cards and no one has seemed to notice, until Jared speaks up. "Fucking newbie over here, with two cards left."

The suit doesn't change all the way around the table, so I'm able to play my queen of diamonds.

There's a chorus of boos.

I put the card facedown on the table, keeping my own face as neutral as possible. Across from me, Morgan narrows his eyes.

If anyone has a two, they get to enact Hunter's rule: a player of their choice has to draw a card. Or a seven, then someone else would get my hand. Briefly, I wonder if Morgan has either, and if he does, would he play it? Or let me win?

We get most of the way around the table when Jared plays a jack—reverse—and it goes around the other way. My heart thuds louder with every play.

Finally it's back to me. Bailey has played an eight of diamonds after drawing four cards—she didn't have another card she could play—so it's my turn.

"Drum roll," Morgan shouts.

Everyone puts their cards down and pounds their hands on the table. The whole thing vibrates with their enthusiasm as I slowly reach for the card to flip it over.

A joker—wild.

"Fuck yes!" Morgan rockets up from his seat and sprints around the table. I'm laughing, giddy, so damn pleased with myself. Morgan reaches me and grabs me, tilting me backward in my seat, over his arms, and plants a deep kiss on my lips.

When he sets me back upright, his friends are laughing and sorting the cards. Jared plunks the trophy and the bag of beers on the table in front of me. "Gonna have a drink now?" he asks, a dark eyebrow curling up.

I glance up at Morgan, who's standing behind me, his hands on my shoulder. He raises an eyebrow and shrugs, leaving it up to me.

"I think I'll hold off."

At six o'clock, hours after the end of Sunday Funday, I swing open the door for On the Rocks. The cowbells clang above me and Grandma glances up at them as we cross the threshold.

"This is it?" she asks, looking around with interest. After lunch and helping her with chores in her apartment, I bundled Grandma up into my Civic and brought her to the bar. The usual crowd is here, including the older ladies in the back booth.

After I won the game and was declared Ruler of the Sirens, we stayed at the top for a while. One by one, the people that had to go to work filtered out, including Morgan. We'd ridden there together knowing he'd have to stay for work and we'd have to find someone to give me a ride. Bailey offered, so Morgan left me at the top of the mountain with a kiss so long and slow someone (probably Jared) threw a strawberry at us. Bailey asked how living together was going and inquired after my grandmother. "You should bring her into town more, so we can meet her," she suggested, and the idea stuck with me.

Today I'd expanded my circle and now I could call some of Morgan's friends my own. Maybe Grandma needed to get outside of her bubble at the retirement community.

Morgan's at the bar, a rag over one shoulder and both his hands on the counter. He's grinning at me, and I get a warm feeling all over.

"What kind of chardonnay do you have?" Grandma asks, without even saying hello.

Morgan rattles off a few names and Grandma complains about a few of them—too oaky, too cheap, too dry—before settling on one.

"Do you want a table?" he asks. "I'll gladly kick someone out for you."

I throw him a look just as Grandma says "please."

"Actually, I was going to introduce Grandma around."

Morgan's eyes dart to the back booth and he nods. "I'll bring your drinks over."

I take Grandma's arm and guide her away from the bar. We arrive at the table where Mrs. Gardiner, Miss Mullins, and Miss Bright are seated. On my best behavior, I make introductions and ask if we can join them.

Politely, they make room for us. Grandma grumbles as she gets into the booth and loudly says, "So this is where you put the old folks."

"Well," Mrs. Gardiner says, affronted.

"I'm seventy-one," Miss Mullins says cheerfully.

"Eighty-three. Ha," Grandma says, like it's a contest. "Where are all the men?"

"Married or dead," Mrs. Gardiner says levelly.

"Small towns have shit dating prospects," Grandma declares.

"You have to keep an open mind," Miss Mullins says.

Miss Bright nods thoughtfully.

"That's why I didn't want to move out here. Small towns are high on drama, low on dating prospects. High on backwoods, narrow-minded rednecks—"

"Now wait just a minute there," Mrs. Gardiner interrupts.

"—low on culture. Hell, I can't even get a good chardonnay in here."

Oh Jesus, this is going off the rails.

Morgan brings us our drinks and my grandmother continues to insult small towns and their residents. His eyes widen and he glances at me.

"Okay, okay, okay," I say over my grandma and Mrs. Gardiner bickering. I have to stand and wave my hands in front of their faces.

Morgan backs away slowly.

Once the women are quiet, I flop back into my seat. "How about this: Morgan and I plan to elope at the courthouse. Discuss."

Four sets of eyes stare at me.

"The courthouse?" Mrs. Gardiner asks, appalled.

"Can you believe it?" my grandmother adds.

"But . . ." Miss Mullins stares at me. "Where will all the Herevians sit?"

"We wouldn't invite anyone."

There's a collective gasp from the three women.

"But I've known Morgan since he was in diapers," Miss Mullins says.

"Is it money?" Mrs. Gardiner leans in.

"No," Grandma bites out. "I cut them a nice check and they insist that they can do whatever they want with it."

"Oh my." Mrs. Gardiner is *scandalized*.

"The courthouse has a lot of history," Miss Mullins allows. "But, oh, dear. It's not the prettiest. There was a roof leak a few years back and the stain is still there."

"A big stain," Miss Bright echoes.

"I tried to tell them to spend at least some of it on a reception. But *noooo*."

"There's a lovely ballroom at Hawthorn," Mrs. Gardiner says.

Grandma hits the tabletop with her palm. "That's where I live. I *told* them!"

"And they don't want to do it there?"

"No!"

They all turn dubious gazes to me, except for Grandma, who studies the three of them. "Did you have kids? Are they married? Where?" she barks out.

And I spend the next half hour listening to four elderly ladies explain to me just how fabulous a small-town wedding in Here could be.

Evil Mermaids

MORGAN

BY THE TIME I GET HOME FROM MY SHIFT RORY'S IN BED with the lights out. She and her grandmother stayed at the bar for a couple of hours, Rory eventually leaving Mrs. Patterson talking with the women while she sat back at the bar near me. Apparently, they found some common ground—Rory said a shared enemy, whoever that might be. She shifts when I crawl in beside her after brushing my teeth and showering.

"Aren't you exhausted?" she asks after a big yawn.

"Bone-dead." Sunday Fundays are long ones, but I wouldn't give up that time with my friends for anything. "What did your grandma think of the bar?"

"She called it a dive." I hear amusement in Rory's voice, her words clearer as she sloughs off her drowsiness.

Well, if she's awake now . . .

I lean in and capture her lips with mine. She makes a noise of surprise but responds quickly, deepening the kiss. I'm too tired to go further, but her lips taste sweet and her body is soft and pliant right now.

We lie facing each other, just like the first night we shared this bed, but the inches between us have shrunk enough that with a tilt of my chin, I can kiss her again.

"Did you drink one of your beers?" I ask.

She smiles against my lips. "No, not yet."

"I'm jealous," I say. "I've never even had one of those. Jared and his dad guard them like the Crown Jewels."

Rory rears back. "Huh. I thought you were going to try to win them for me."

"Oh I totally was."

"If you'd won you could have had them all yourself."

"Eh, I would have shared it with you." I pause. "Maybe."

She chuckles. "Well, lucky for you I'm in a sharing mood."

"A sharing mood, eh?" I laugh into another kiss and slide her leg up my hip. Her skin is hot and soft, and my fingers trace lazy circles while we make out.

When we finally break apart enough to talk again, Rory continues. "Do you have to work tomorrow?"

I sigh. With leaves approaching peak fall colors, the rentals are fully booked out over the weekends. "Yeah. Another early morning with Kit. Three houses to clean, but I'll be done in the afternoon."

"Well." Her lips shift down and she kisses my chin before burrowing into my arms. "What if we had a picnic tomorrow night?"

OF COURSE, I KNOW EXACTLY WHERE I'M GOING TO TAKE her. I call in Hunter to run the lift again for us—"Sure, it's not like I have a life," he teases—and we take Rory's hard-won beers and a couple bags of food up to the top.

I got home after working with Kit and showered before taking Princess out to the backyard with me. We played for a while, leaving Rory alone to get her work done. Then I took a nap on the couch and woke up to Barty loafing on my chest and Rory gazing at me with a mixture of amusement and fondness.

When she wrapped up around five I had everything packed up and ready to go. Hunter ran the lift for us while we rode up to the top.

"Huh, look at that; the view's still gorgeous," she says as we stand by the picnic table and gaze down at the valley. We've made it up quickly enough that there's still an hour till sunset, and the weather is on the warm side for October, though we're both wearing jeans and light jackets. I've got blankets and a heavier coat so we can stay as long as possible.

"Your domain, my queen," I tease. For a moment on the chairlift, I wondered if I should take her somewhere different.

But Sirens is clearly the best place around. There's no view like it, and there will be no one else up here but us. Down in town the leaf peepers—or at least, the ones willing to visit on the weekdays—will be walking the trails, eating in the few restaurants that are open, and keeping the town in a brief blaze of busyness for another week or so, although there's a rainstorm in the forecast for Friday, and it's likely that the leaves will be mostly blown down before the weekend.

We don't sit at the table; instead I spread a blanket down even closer to the edge of the run and pull out the beers. "My queen?" I offer, and Rory deadpans a royal nod.

I settle in beside her and crack each beer open. She takes one from me and I tip my bottle toward her. "You've won the game, won your crown, and won my friends." *And won my heart*, I think. "Congratulations."

We clink and take a long pull from our beers. The pilsner is crisp and hoppy, and Rory moans in pleasure.

"Holy shit," she says.

"Hell yeah," I agree. "Jared and his dad know their beers."

Rory takes another swallow. "How involved is Jared in the brewery?"

"Very," I say. "His old man's getting up in years and Jared runs things now."

"Is he single?" Rory asks. She's sitting cross-legged, her dark hair tumbling around her shoulders and outlining her face against the sky.

"What? One sip of his beer and you're ready to jump ship on me?" I tease.

Rory laughs and nudges me. "I meant the dad. For Grandma."

I roll down to my side and prop my head up on one hand. "Nah, still happily married. I didn't realize you were matchmaking."

Rory rolls her eyes. "She says that *I* need to get laid, which—"

"Check. Done. Mission accomplished. We can keep the orgasm supply rolling."

"—*which* is no longer the case, and I wonder if she's

been projecting all this time." Rory and I both drop our laughter. "She always says she wants a younger man who can keep up with her, but I wonder sometimes if that's really what she wants. Or if . . ."

Rory goes quiet. I take another sip of my beer—god, it's good—and let her gather her thoughts.

"I wonder if what she really means is that she wants someone younger so that maybe they'll outlive her and won't have to face being left again."

I peer up at Rory. She's looking out over the view, the miles and miles of reds, oranges, and golds stretching out below us. I put a hand on her knee and squeeze. It pulls her out enough that she glances at me, attempts a weak smile, and changes the subject. "Hey, I was wondering; why is it called Sirens Valley?"

"Ah, good question." I sit up and cross my ankles before dragging the paper bag close and pulling out the food. "What do you know of sirens?"

"Evil mermaids?"

I grin. "That's what most people think of. But the original sirens were winged creatures. Original, as in, Homer's *Odyssey* and before," I add, opening up a container of mixed olives. "Back in 'ye olden times' here, hunters and trappers in this region would swear that they heard women singing. The ghost stories were all vague and varied until 1842, when the town was all about lumber and a young, strapping bachelor went missing. Then the story turned to sirens, because who else would snatch up a handsome man? But two days later his body floated down the river, and it turns out he was holding a girl hostage in his cabin. And then people started to wonder if maybe it really was sirens, saving the girl's life. Scary, lethal, beautiful . . . but ultimately, saviors. The legend stuck."

"So the legend is that sirens inhabit these woods and

rescue fair maidens?" The corner of her mouth tips up in a smirk.

"Well, I *have* heard the song."

Rory's smirk fades as she realizes I'm serious. Then it shifts to skepticism. "You believe in sirens?"

I shrug. "Sometimes I think there's something about the shape of the valley and the way the wind blows through it. But I've heard—or maybe felt is a better word—the song of this place." I pause, a tub of hummus in my hands, and look out over the valley. "There's something that calls to people here. It might be a song. Something we can't really hear, but feel."

I take the lid off the hummus and set it down on the blanket. Then I fish out a bag of pita chips and tear it open. "Anyway, the lodge was opened in the sixties as an attempt to revive tourism in the Catskills, and the legends persisted enough to stick it with the name."

Rory raises an eyebrow. "And the rest is history?"

I grin. "Exactly."

We eat our meal and watch the way the sun plays over the valley. I finish my beer, and so does Rory. She cracks open the last two and hands me one. I pack up the leftovers and crawl around to sit behind her. She leans against me, my spread knees caging her in. She rests her left hand on my knee, and the diamond glows in the warm light.

"Where did you get this ring?"

I smile into her hair. I'm surprised it took so long to ask, but Rory hasn't exactly been as open to me as she is now—or as inquisitive. "It was my grandmother's."

Rory's quiet a beat and then sits bolt upright. "Wait, what? *Your grandmother's?*"

I lean back on one hand, smirking at her. "Yeah."

"Morgan . . ." She stares at me. "Is this diamond real?"

"Yup."

"You put a family heirloom on the finger of a total stranger? Do I want to know how much this is worth?"

"Yes and no."

"Morgan. What the hell? You trust me with this?"

The question sobers me, and I give her the brutally honest answer. "I trust you with a lot of things, Rory Fox." *Like my heart.*

A Two-to-One Ratio

RORY

I LAUNCH MYSELF AT MORGAN AND HE CATCHES ME WITH A grunt, banding an arm around my waist and meeting my kiss with as much ferocity as I give him. He sits us up straighter as I climb into his lap, wrapping my arms around his neck and squeezing his hips with my knees.

The air is cooling but he's like a furnace underneath me, his mouth hot and hard and taking long, slow pulls from mine. We're *drinking* each other, much like we did with the beers, and I think, *ha, best thing I've ever had in my mouth.*

My hands move from Morgan's hair to his face, cupping his jaw and enjoying the bristle of his scruff against my palms. Morgan's hands move under my shirt, spots of heat sweeping around until I'm pulled tight against him. I widen my legs and press our groins together.

We both moan.

"We're alone up here, right?"

"Yeah," he says, barely pulling his mouth away from mine. "You can be as loud as you want. As loud as I'm going to make you."

My belly flips and we resume kissing. I grind against his erection, my rocking building more and more until I run out of room and push Morgan down onto the blanket. He goes willingly, eyes sparkling up at me. "Please tell me you want to sit on my face again."

"I had other things in mind." I brace myself over him and kiss him again.

"Oh?" he says between kisses.

"Yeah. I have a condom."

He laughs and I accidentally kiss his teeth. "I do too. We can do both things."

I move down his body, since I'm on top. We pull the Henley over his head, giving me access to the smooth expanse of his chest. I kiss the tattoos, enjoying the way his chest rises and falls with every hitch of his breath.

"Rory . . ." he mutters when I get to his belt and start to undo it. I pull and he lifts his hips and the moment his clothes are down far enough I suck the head of his cock into my mouth. "Jesus. Fuck!"

My hair has fallen over my face and Morgan scoops it up into a fist and holds it lightly back so he can see. I swirl my tongue around the head of his cock and glance up at him. He's wild-eyed, teeth gritted and muscles rippling.

"We can do both things," he repeats, chest heaving. "But not all things, Rory."

I pull my mouth off his cock with a pop. "Just a bit more."

He groans and his head falls back. I suck him in again, taking him as deep as I can over and over. His thighs tighten under my palms and his legs squirm. The taste of precum floods my mouth and his hand tightens in my hair.

"Rory, please, fuck stop, oh god."

I pull off and the hand that was gripping my hair shifts to squeeze his cock head. Morgan's knees bend, his body curling up to try to stave off the orgasm I teased. He mutters a few more curse words, and then it's "Rory, *please* get on my face."

I oblige, stripping off my clothes and crawling naked up his body to his eagerly waiting mouth. He pulls me down hard and knowing what he can take, I sink onto him.

It doesn't take long for me to grind against him, riding his tongue until an orgasm barrels up my body from my toes to my head, escaping in a near scream while I pulse and shudder over him. I fall back to sit on his chest and catch my breath.

Morgan grabs a napkin, wiping his mouth, and then grabs his jeans, fishing a condom out of the wallet. His hands disappear behind me and I hear the rip of the packet and watch Morgan's hooded eyes while he rolls the condom on.

Wordlessly, he touches my waist and I rise up, centering myself on him and slowly lowering. We both pause when I bottom out, the stretch and depth hitting me just right. Through half-lidded eyes, I watch Morgan's tortured gaze stare up at the sky while he fights for control.

"God damn it," he says, breaking and laughing at himself. "This is not going to last long. You'll probably set me off if you come."

"I really want you to make me come again."

"Fuck yeah." Morgan sucks a thumb into his mouth and presses it to my clit, shooting fireworks up my body. My hands scramble to find purchase, one landing on his bent knee behind me, the other on his chest. "God, Rory, you are so beautiful."

I close my eyes and throw my head back, grinding myself on his cock. His thumb circles my clit over and over again. This orgasm takes me longer, and the noises Morgan makes sound like I'm killing him. The ache builds and I can feel it approaching. I lean back and open my eyes, meeting Morgan's gaze. "I'm getting close," I gasp, and the words themselves spur me on even more.

Morgan licks his other thumb and switches, and the renewed pressure takes me over the edge. My toes curl and my orgasm shakes through me. Morgan's hips grind with me as he pulses inside me. We're both panting, and when I lift my hand off his chest to brush my hair away from my face, it's shaking.

Morgan cracks an eye open, and then stretches his arms out to me. I ease myself down onto his chest. We're both sweaty, but it's cooling quickly in the autumn breeze, and the sun's almost gone. It's going to get cold fast.

I'm too satiated to do anything about that yet. Morgan feels too good. He smells good too, and I press my nose against his skin, against the wings tattooed on his pec. I bet—

"Did you just bite me?" he asks, voice filled with laughter.

I bite him again, this time holding it. "Wha?" I ask, my voice completely muffled. "Ew tast gud."

"I taste good?" His chest bounces, and I let go, resting my chin on his sternum. Morgan's got one arm wrapped around me, the other behind his head. "You can bite me anytime, my little vampire queen."

I laugh, and this time it pushes his softening cock out of me. We reluctantly sit up and clean ourselves, Morgan putting the used condom into the empty chip bag. He lies back down but I take a moment to admire the view—of Morgan, yes, but also the valley.

It's beautiful, and I liked hearing the lore of this place, but that's all it is—lore. I don't believe that there's a song, I don't feel anything pulling me to the valley like Morgan does.

Despite the slogan, I don't belong here, even if I am fucking my fake fiancé.

I lie back down on the blanket and Morgan trails a hand up my already-goose-bumped skin.

"Getting cold?"

I nod.

"Cold enough that you want to go?"

I shake my head. "We still have another condom," I point out.

He bends his head and kisses my hip. "That would help us stay warm." He shifts and pulls his jeans up and buttons them. Then he reaches for his shirt and I frown in disappointment until he hands it to me. "Here, put this on."

I pull the Henley on and lie back down. Morgan's eyes run appreciatively over my half-naked body, and then his hand follows the path, coming to rest between my legs. I'm still slick and swollen, and he traces my lips up to my clit and back down the other side, making my head fall back.

"What do you aim for, a two-to-one ratio?" I tease.

"I can absolutely make you come two more times before me."

"That makes you an anomaly among men," I say, breath catching when he circles my clit. His eyes are watching his fingers. "You'd be shocked how many guys I've been with who've considered the night over without even one orgasm for me."

"I would not be shocked. I was one of those guys back in my youth. Mostly because I didn't have a fucking clue what I was doing in the beginning, just too eager to get my rocks off."

I snort at the euphemism, and Morgan retaliates with a hard circle on my clit before he backs off.

"Being a bartender in a small ski town has its perks," he continues. He glances up to meet my gaze. "Do you want to hear this? Or would you prefer not to know about my past?"

"Tell me." I don't even hesitate. I want to know what made Morgan who he is.

"Well, back when I was a young hotshot," he says, in a mocking tone, "I happened to take a woman home from the bar who was maybe a decade older than me. I finished and she looked at me and said, 'That's it?' and boy, if that isn't a hit to a man's ego."

I shift my hips. Morgan's light touch on my body is building me up in this achingly slow torture. The corner of his mouth lifts in a smile and he knows exactly what he's doing.

"No one had ever complained, but now I realize that most women don't realize they *should* complain. The bar for guys is so fucking low. So I made it my mission to single-handedly tackle the orgasm gap." He chuckles, and it's self-deprecating. Then his eyes twinkle. "That and I really fucking like eating pussy."

I close my eyes and tilt my head back. Even through the building haze of an impending orgasm, I can see it. Morgan's so desperate to be loved, to be wanted. It shows in the way he charms everyone, even the most difficult people, like my grandmother. It's how he broke through my defenses, even when I didn't want to let anyone in.

"I'm not going to complain about your sex-god origin story," I gasp out, and he laughs.

I feel the blanket beneath me tug and then Morgan's

warm breath on my neck as he kisses the hollow. His thumb replaces his fingers and he circles my entrance. I spread my legs even farther and he pushes in. His pinkie and pointer slide down the seam of my legs while his middle two fingers curl inside me.

"I love the way you move," he says into my skin. "The way you ride my cock, my tongue. The way you're riding my hand."

Before it was teasing, now he's determined. He finds just the right spot inside me, driving me wild from both sides. When my hips rise up, his other arm snakes behind me, keeping me lifted. He moves his whole hand, thumb against my clit, fingers fucking into me. It's rough and aggressive and it drives me right up and over the edge until I'm crying out and clamping down on his hand. He doesn't stop until I push him away.

Morgan disappears, and I swipe the back of my hand over my forehead, wiping away the sheen of sweat. The sky is a deep indigo now, the first stars popping out above us. There's the crinkle of the condom wrapper and then Morgan's back, easing inside me, and this time is slow and steady, Morgan holding himself above me, kissing me, until the sky is full of stars and we're both completely spent.

I Only Have You

RORY

It's *supposed* to be an easy week for me. I don't have to drive anywhere until Wednesday, so I have an extra day with Morgan. Not that long ago I would have been spending my extra time with Grandma, and I feel a twinge of guilt in my gut before I remind myself that Grandma and I need a life outside of each other. We need friends, and even if Morgan is a fake fiancé, something about this feels real.

The night we spent up on the mountain unleashed something insatiable, because I spend Tuesday morning not working and instead we completely scandalize both pets by fucking all over the house until Morgan has to leave to open the bar.

Wednesday I drive to Long Island and the repair I'm supposed to work on goes sideways. I am out on the line

Thursday night, keeping both me and my software guy working late, and the solution evades us until Saturday afternoon, so I'm late getting back to Here and I pull into On the Rocks at its busiest to give Morgan a quick hello and wolf down some tots while sitting out in the back—the only place with free seats because it's getting too cold.

I'm asleep before Morgan gets home that night, but in the morning, as I try to slip out, he pulls me back into bed, facedown, and crawls on top of me. We break out one of the vibrators and I come around his cock while he spreads my ass cheeks and watches.

My post-orgasm bliss doesn't last very long though, because I go alone to Grandma's apartment and she's in a foul mood. We have lunch and she complains about *everything* and gets in a fight with a woman at the table next to us, which ends in her making a rude gesture and me dragging us both out before management can come and deal with her.

The last thing I need is for her to get kicked out of a very expensive community. I bet they don't refund your deposit if you have to leave for bad behavior.

Not that Grandma has to worry about getting her deposit back. Today is one of the checkbook balancing days, and that always culminates in us reviewing her investments too—is she sweeping enough income into her checking to cover her living expenses? Do we need to move money in or out?

I hesitate. Grandma's bank balance has been unusually high for the past few months because there's one outstanding check that's waiting to be cashed—mine.

"What?" Grandma bites out. We're sitting side by side at her computer, as usual, with Grandma watching over my shoulder even though she can't see much because her glasses are on top of her head and her eyesight is gradually getting worse. Honestly, I'm not sure why she has a computer anymore. I've restricted a lot of it to try to avoid her accidentally clicking on things, but at some point it might just be easier to switch to one of those simple tablets for kids and the elderly.

"Nothing," I say.

Grandma's been here for five months now, and this lie that Morgan and I have told is going to have to resolve somehow. When we cooked up this scheme, I was only thinking about getting Grandma off my back about being single and alone. But now, I wonder how long we can keep it going. Could Morgan be the reason we stay in Here? Is that what I want?

"You haven't cashed the check yet." Grandma's words have a finality to it. She already knows, and her voice holds the early warning signs I remember as a kid, the portender of getting in trouble. "It could be doing you some good. By now it should have been used to make a deposit on the venue, or a caterer, or even if you elope, at least it could have bought you a nice dress and a photographer. But instead that money sits in my bank account doing nothing because you never intended to marry Morgan at all!"

Grandma gets up and grabs her cane, pacing to the far wall.

"That's . . . it's just a lot of money, that's all."

She gives me the stink eye at my weak excuse and hobbles toward me. "Here's what I think. I think you've set this whole thing up so I would feel like I have to stay here. I've seen *The Proposal*. You fake an engagement and both get something you want. You get a reason to keep me here in Here"—she scoffs—"what did Morgan get out of it? What was so worth the annoyance of coming here and putting up with me, hmm?"

Before I can open my mouth for a rebuttal, Grandma

points a finger at me. "You probably still have your own apartment, don't you?"

This time, she expects an answer. "Yes. But——"

"This was a lie from the beginning. Of course it was moving fast, you even said so yourself, but I thought I'd give you the benefit of the doubt. I thought maybe, I could push you to either fall in love or come clean. So here we are, almost two months later, and don't you dare lie to me again, Lorelai Evelyn Fox. Are you going to marry Morgan?"

I stare at my grandma, her finger pointing at me accusingly, and my stomach sinks. Would she even believe me if I lied again? And if I did lie, then what? What is my actual plan?

Would this conversation be going differently if Morgan was here? Would he be his usual, charming self, and have defused my grandmother's mood before it got to this point?

But then, I'm glad he's not here. Because I'd be putting him on the spot. We've only *just* started sleeping together, and no man wants the grandmother of the woman he's sleeping with to be staring at him, daring him to say that he's going to keep the lie up.

"No, I'm not going to marry Morgan."

We stare at each other for a moment until Grandma's hand falls back to her side. "Well then," she says, and I avert my gaze. "That settles that. There's a place outside of Boston that I've been in touch with and I'll reach out to see how that wait-list is going."

Grandma's voice has changed, shifted. I've defused the bomb, but not in the right way. I've caused irreparable damage, which is further inflicted when Grandma says, "Don't lie to me like that again, Rory. You have your job and your life outside of mine, but I only have you."

Doomed from
the Start

MORGAN

RORY DOESN'T COME INTO THE BAR AFTER VISITING HER grandma, though she does message the group text with me and my neighbor to tell us she's home and she'll take care of Princess tonight.

The bar's decently busy—the last gasp of leaf peepers. It's been a long peak this year, since the forecasted rain held off. Two years ago, the leaves peaked on a Wednesday and a storm rolled through Friday morning, blowing the red, orange, and yellow leaves through the streets like party confetti. Next we'll have a big lull until the temperature drops enough to make snow and the ski season starts.

It's not just locals though—Kit's here, too, and he brought a woman in with him. It takes me a minute to realize who it is—name redacted so I don't get sued—but she's wearing enough of a disguise that I only recognize her because I know she's in town. No one else would look twice at her and think, "Oh my god, isn't she famous for—"

Shit. I probably gave too much away.

Anyhoo, they're sitting with Hunter, and I wonder if Hunter has any clue who he's talking to.

I worry about Kit, though. The more I watch them the more I think there's something there, and if there is, it's bound to be doomed. Why would she even be in Here, New York? It makes no sense.

I shake my head at myself. I do believe that everyone belongs Here, just like our town motto claims, but that might be stretching it too far. I'm lucky to have found Rory.

The night wraps up and I go home. Barty greets me with a soft meow from his loaf on the kitchen island and I get ready for bed as quietly as possible, discovering Princess lying on the comforter with Rory.

Not for long.

Rory rolls over to me and she's so warm and soft in her sleepiness, and after a few kisses, Princess hops off the bed in a huff while I get on my knees on the floor and drag Rory's ass to the edge.

With our schedules so different, we might have to get used to sleepy sex. I throw Rory's legs over my shoulders and I'm not even sure she mutters a coherent word or has opened her eyes before a quiet, shuddering orgasm takes over her body.

I crawl up the bed and pull her toward me. "Go back to sleep," I whisper in her ear. But she doesn't. She pulls me to her and then reaches across to the nightstand, fumbling for a condom. She puts it on and I enter her, rocking slow and steady, her leg thrown over my hip. We're connected, mouth, chest, hips. Legs tangled. Fingers knotted together.

I don't do a good job keeping it together, mostly because Rory refuses to let go of my hand so I can play with her clit and give her another orgasm. Mine rolls over me in waves, and I press deep inside her as I come.

Rory rolls off the bed to clean up, and I feel bad that she's had to wake up enough to clean up. But she was the one that grabbed the condom, and, boy, I am *not* turning her down.

When she's done, I clean up too and then get back into bed. Princess is snoring from the floor and Rory's curled up on her side. I let her sleep, carefully draping an arm over her and vowing to make up for the missing orgasm in the morning.

WHEN I GET UP IN THE *ACTUAL* DAYLIGHT-INFUSED morning, the bed is empty. Princess is curled up by the door looking at me expectantly, waiting to be let out.

I let her out in the backyard and go to the bathroom myself. The house is quiet, Rory's not home.

I let Princess in and walk through the den back into the kitchen. Then I stop. I retrace my steps, backing up until I can see the corner of the den where Bartholomeow's litter box should be sitting.

It's not there.

I take a brisk walk through the house now, more awake than before. "Barty?" I call out. He typically hides in the mornings, more of a night owl cat than a morning cat. But all his stuff is gone.

I text Rory.

My Queen

Where's Barty?

She doesn't respond right away so I put my phone down and feed Princess, making breakfast for myself, too.

Soon a car door slams and Rory stomps up to the back door.

I put my spoon down. "Hey."

"Hey," she returns, hands in her pockets. Rory bites her lip.

"Where's Barty?" My heartbeat has picked up, a feeling of dread hitting my gut. My gut is dramatic as hell.

I hope.

"I took him back to Grandma's. We had a talk yesterday and . . . well." Her eyes are down on her shoes. "I'm sorry." She finally looks up at me and her eyes are bright.

"Why?"

She takes her hands out of her pocket and looks down at the ring on her finger. It catches the light, and she runs the finger of her opposite hand over it, around the band before gripping it and pulling it off.

"I never should have said yes to your proposal. It was reckless and stupid, and now Grandma's found out about our lie and she's pissed. She's also . . . she's moving to Boston."

Rory holds the ring out toward me. I don't take it.

She steps forward and sets the ring on the kitchen island between us. My stomach drops as she says, "I'm going with her."

Her hands go back in her pockets and we both stare at the ring. I move toward her, but she holds up her hand. "Don't. I just . . . I promised her that she had to give it six months, and those six months are nearly up, and now I have to move with her. And this way"—she gestures toward the ring—"you can do that thing with your friends to buy the ski place."

"I'd rather have you than this diamond ring. I'd rather have you than the lodge."

Rory breaks, her eyes flashing with pent-up emotions. It's not the ideal response, I'll admit. "Don't say that!" she shouts at me, throwing her hands to the side. "Grandma is the only family I have. She loves me, albeit in her own way, and I lied to her."

Rory takes a deep, shuddering breath. "So now I'm going to go pack my things. I don't know when Grandma's going to be able to move, but at least my stuff will be all in one place and I don't have to—" She cuts herself off.

She doesn't have to what? Be with me?

There's a honk from the driveway. *Shit.* It's Kit coming to pick me up for a cleaning job. I groan out loud, squeezing my eyes shut. When I open them again, Rory's gone, and I can hear her packing her things up in the guest room.

Princess whines and I look out the window at Kit in the driveway. He waves.

"Gimme two," I say, holding up two fingers. He nods.

I dart to my room and throw some jeans on. This is a regular cleaning job, not a washboard one, so I shout at Rory, hopping on one leg and then the other. "Let's talk about this."

"If you figure out how to teleport to Boston to see me, sure."

"We can do long distance. It's like . . . three hours away."

"You work seven days a week."

"I'll quit my job," I impulsively shout. I grab a clean shirt from the laundry pile and throw it on.

Rory doesn't respond for a moment, and when I finish pulling my socks on, she's standing in the doorway. "Then you'll never get your own bar and you'll leave your best friend in the lurch. I live wherever Grandma is, and you live here. Face it, our fake engagement was doomed from the start."

The Wrong Question

RORY

THE NEXT FEW WEEKS ARE A PARTICULAR KIND OF HELL. I interview pet sitters and hire someone to come take care of Bartholomeow once a day to help Grandma. His coat stays clean, but my heart twinges every time I think about how I'd look up from my work when Morgan was home and would find Barty loafing on his chest, Morgan absentmindedly petting him.

Grandma puts an ungodly amount of money down for a deposit on her new place in Boston and I move back to my place in Westchester.

All that happens between jobs, and I go back to my visiting-every-other-week schedule. It feels lonelier than it did before.

I don't go to On the Rocks on Sunday nights. I haven't

seen Morgan since I left. We've only talked via text to sort out when I could come by and get my stuff.

He didn't once call me "my queen" and I felt like I was talking to a completely different person—like Morgan had given up on trying to charm me.

I hated it.

Finally, Grandma's moving day is approaching. I'm spending the weekend with her and the movers will be here tomorrow, Monday. We spent all day Saturday packing up her kitchen and bathroom, and today we've tackled the bedroom and living room. It's been slow going, wrapping each picture frame, folding all the clothes. Grandma took an extra-long nap, and now we're down to the wire. It's dark outside, and the movers come at 8 a.m.

Bartholomeow winds around my ankle. "Grandma? Do you remember where we put your laptop bag?" She's moved four times, and I'm just thankful she doesn't have a desktop.

"The front hall closet," she says, with a lot of confidence for a woman who misplaced her cane and had to take her backup one to lunch yesterday.

I get up to retrieve it and Bartholomeow voices his complaints.

"I think he misses Morgan," Grandma says.

I ignore her. She's brought up Morgan several times and I get madder each and every time.

"Rory? Don't you think he misses Morgan?"

"Of course he does," I mutter. "He's a cat. And Morgan was a nice warm person who cuddled with him and fed him and pretty much loved on him but also gave Barty his space when he needed it."

Grandma doesn't respond. When I glance over, Bartholomeow is on her lap and she's giving me a funny look.

I ignore her.

We sit in silence while I pack up her cords and mousepad. I really should be cleaning the keyboard before I put it in, but I think we already packed up the compressed air somewhere.

"Rory, I'm sorry."

My hands freeze.

Grandma continues. "Sometimes I . . ." She searches for the right word, and I look up at her. "Your mother said I was manipulative. I'll never forget the argument we had where she said that." Grandma's hands come to rest on her cane and Barty's ears twitch. I can almost see him debating whether it's worth staying where he is if he's not going to get pets. "I wasn't a good grandmother."

I open my mouth to protest and she raises her hand to stop me.

"I wasn't a good grandmother when your mother was alive." She sighs. "I thought I knew everything about how to be a mother, and it wasn't until I took you into my care that I realized I had no goddamn idea on how to raise a child anymore. Maybe it gets harder with every generation. I don't know. But when I realized you had lied to me— manipulated me—I thought some terrible, awful things about the both of us and I lashed out. For that, I'm sorry."

I sit on that for a moment. When I was growing up I had asked Grandma why she and Mom hadn't been close, and she'd been vague. "We didn't see eye to eye on things," she'd said. "But even though we disagreed, I should have mended fences more, swallowed my own pride. It's a lesson for us both." She reached out and touched my cheek. "It's a lesson that life is short and even when our tempers get the best of us, we should reach out anyway. Forgive."

I blink the memory away. I look at Grandma. "For what it's worth, I'm sorry too."

Grandma reaches out and I grab her hand. And then she gets to her real point. "Do *you* miss Morgan?"

I close my eyes. "What does it matter?"

Grandma lets go of my hand and chuckles. "Oh, Rory. I've been a fool. I asked you the wrong question, didn't I?"

I open my eyes and look at her. "What do you mean?"

She purses her lips and looks at me. "I asked if you were going to marry him. But maybe I should have asked if you love him?"

"It doesn't matter, Grandma. You're not happy here, and we're moving to Boston."

She harrumphs and points at her top drawer. "Open that up and pull out the papers."

I oblige, closing the drawer and sitting back with the thick stack. I glance at the top one. It's an email printed out. "You know how to print out emails?" I ask.

"Jenny down at the tech hour showed me how to print from my phone. And she showed me how to make the text extra large too."

It is extra large, and there's only a few lines per page—no wonder the stack is so thick. There's only one line of the actual email on this page below the header.

My eyes snag on the sender. *Janet Mullins.*

Dear Valerie,

It was lovely to see you Tuesday and the preserve appreciates your donation to the pre-K program. Those kids will keep us young! You should come spend time with us again next week.

-J (she/her)

I leaf to the next page. An email from someone named mrsgardineronwisterialane, no salutations:

Valerie,

Shall we visit the Italian restaurant next? Or the horse farm? How do you think Rory would feel about an outdoor wedding?

Depends on the season, I suppose. If they decide to marry in April it's better to be cautious.

I'll pick you up at two.

It's unsigned, but I can guess.

I thumb through the pages, my eye catching on the "from" row, and I discover group emails, threads of making plans, and getting-to-know-you conversations.

"Why didn't you tell me you were spending time with these women?"

Grandma sighs. "At first we were discussing your wedding plans. I didn't want to seem like I was pushing you two to commit, and I certainly didn't want to come off as demanding how you spend the money I gave you again. And then . . ." She shrugs. "I started having fun."

I finally make it to the last page, and a line catches my eye.

I'm so glad Morgan connected us via email.

Morgan did this? He found my grandmother some friends?

"You didn't answer my question." Grandma thumps her cane on the floor, leaning in and dislodging Barty, who yowls in indignation and runs into the back hallway. "Do you love him?"

I stare at the papers in my hand.

We don't make sense, at all. Morgan's charming, friendly—hell, he's even a dog person. I'm not any of those things—okay, maybe Princess has convinced me that dogs are pretty awesome. But I can't ski, I don't want to make friends with all two thousand Herevians, I don't know the lore of the Catskills, I don't have a relationship with my elementary school teacher, and I definitely don't hear the song of the place like Morgan does.

But when we're together, I realize—I *want* it. I want that belonging. I want that sense of community, that group of friends that's willing to pool their money for the benefit of everyone.

And mostly, I want Morgan. I could never be that person without him.

"Yes," I say, looking back up at my grandmother. "I love him."

She slaps her knee. "Well, then you have my blessing to go get him."

"But what about you? You don't like it here."

She waves my concern away. "It's true that I don't like it here in the independent living community. But I like Here. Who knows, maybe I can convince Janet to move into a house with me and we can hire twenty-four-seven care and form a commune."

I raise an eyebrow. "As in . . . a lover?"

"Good grief. I like the woman, but not enough to give up my hopes and dreams of snagging a younger man. And you know I like the di—"

"Stop!" I cry, throwing up my hands. I get to my feet. "And with that thought, I'm going to go talk to Morgan."

Grandma looks smugly at me. "Good. You know what those Herevians say, don't you?"

"You belong Here," we say together.

For the first time, I think that just might be true.

My Knees Are
Weak

RORY

I zoom along the road from Grandma's place to On the Rocks, glad that it's later than I normally show up and maybe the bar will be less crowded, quieter, and we can have an actual conversation.

It's a cold night and I'm glad I threw another layer under my leather jacket. Of course, I have my gloves and boots on, cutting the chill down further.

The moon is out, bright and full ahead of me, and the street is fairly empty. One of the big turns is coming up, and I reach for the brake on the right handlebar, only to find air instead, and my stomach drops.

I fumble, reaching out, thinking *for sure* the brake is there somewhere, but it's not. I break into a cold sweat and belatedly hit the pedal on the right foot peg, triggering the rear brake. It's there, thank god, but because of the delay

I'm now taking the turn too quickly and just barely manage to stay upright. The rear brake isn't as powerful as the front brake, and I almost have too much momentum.

I slow, pulling over to the shoulder and easing to a stop. My knee jitters, and I don't think I'm going to be able to hold the bike upright so I quickly engage the stand and hop off.

Yup, my knees are weak, I'm sweating under my clothes, and I feel like I can't breathe.

That could have been bad—really bad. If I'd flown off the road at the curve, who knows how long it would have been until someone had found me. Morgan wasn't expecting me, Grandma might assume I'd be gone all night.

I rip my helmet off and put my hands on my knees, taking big, gulping inhales of air. *Did that really just happen?* Even though the adrenaline that's coursing through me is sharp and unpleasant, I still straighten up, grab my phone from my jacket pocket, and turn on the light. The brake handle can't be gone. I've heard of this happening once before, but it was a mechanic's error and I haven't had anyone else touch my bike in ages. How would that have happened?

Maybe it's because my flashlight is on, blinding me. Or maybe it's that my bike is still on, the engine noise covering all other sounds up.

Either way, I don't see the dark vehicle coming at me until it's too late.

Alibi

Morgan

There are three people left in the bar—one couple from out of town and a loner who makes me think of Rory, even though he's a grumpy mid-fifties Latino.

I haven't been having the best day. Or week, for that matter.

I miss Rory. Her stuff is gone, and Barty's gone too. Princess is sad, moping around the house. But maybe she's feeding off my energy.

My friends can tell too. Kit came by earlier to give me a big hug and Hunter's been behind the bar with me. He told me to go home, but I didn't want to. Maybe it was some ridiculous hope that Rory would still show up after visiting her grandmother.

To pass the time until the guests leave, Hunter and I play darts.

"With you joining the lodge, that makes five. I'm still hopeful that Kit will join somehow," Hunter says.

Last week, I sold the ring. I contacted a few of the closest jewelers and the first one that got back to me drove all the way up here to buy the ring from me. So now I'm flush with cash and am a proud new member of the group chat for buying the lodge.

Yay.

Can't you feel my enthusiasm?

"Uh-huh," I say, so Hunter will keep talking. He's excited, and I like that my friend has found an outlet for all his energy, aside from wrangling our generation of Herevians into backyard barbecues and Sunday Funday brunches. He's been a great boss, and I don't want that part of our relationship to end.

He drones on about setting up co-op paperwork and the idea of throwing a new ownership party at the top of Sirens Valley.

My phone rings in my back pocket and I ignore it. I'm not expecting any calls, I don't really want to talk to anyone, and it's my turn anyway and I need two sixteens and a twenty.

The phone stops ringing, I nail the double sixteen, and the phone starts up again. I retrieve the darts with one hand and pull out my phone with the other.

It's Rory's grandmother.

"Hello?"

"Morgan?" There's something urgent and wild in her tone that has the hairs on the back of my neck rising.

"Yeah?"

"Rory's in the hospital after a hit-and-run. Come pick me up. Right now, Morgan!"

She hangs up before I can fully process what she says, and then I turn to Hunter, my eyes wide. "I gotta go."

THERE'S NO BARGING THROUGH THE DOOR SHOUTING, "Where is she!" Instead, I trot after Mrs. Patterson, who's plowing along with her cane while her voice wobbles with emotions. We get directed down the hall after verifying that Mrs. Patterson is Rory's next of kin, and weave through the maze of rooms and curtains until a nurse pulls one aside and there she is.

"Oh," Rory's grandmother says next to me, and that one word is infused with so much. Rory's eyes are closed and she's lying prone in the hospital bed. Staff buzz around her.

Her face is . . . her face is bad. There's road rash on one side and dried blood on her chin and lips. Her nose looks wrong, and her loose hair has grass and gravel in it.

My heart feels like it's in the wrong place, like I misplaced it weeks ago and have been looking for it. Like the beeping of the machine Rory's hooked up to is my heartbeat, not hers.

How could I have let Rory go without fighting harder?

"Valerie Patterson?"

I glance over and there's a doctor beside us, consulting paperwork on a clipboard. Mrs. Patterson hasn't made a sound yet, and the look on her face can only be described as devastation. She lost her daughter, Rory's mother, years ago, and now she might lose her granddaughter.

I swallow thickly. "Yes, that's her." I carefully touch Mrs. Patterson's elbow and direct her attention away from Rory.

The doctor continues. "Your granddaughter is lucky she was found so quickly. I know it looks bad, but she's sedated right now while we prep her to set the bone. She has a broken tibia, and obviously you can see the damage to her face—"

"Wasn't she wearing her helmet?" Mrs. Patterson interrupts.

The doctor hesitates. "Her helmet was nearby, but she wasn't wearing it at the time of impact. The police will be checking in once we get her stabilized and awake to try to piece together what happened. But for now, what you need to know is that her injuries only look bad. We don't detect any internal bleeding. She's in good hands, and we'll get her sorted."

The nurses start to wheel her bed out to the hallway but Mrs. Patterson shouts, "Wait!" And moves to her bedside. The nurses stop, and Mrs. Patterson briefly sets her hand in her granddaughter's and squeezes. After a few seconds, she pats the hand and lets them move on. "Thank you," she tells the staff.

WE WAIT. I PACE OFTEN, WONDERING IF I SHOULD EVEN BE here—if Rory even wants me here. But I admit that I just can't be anywhere else right now. The woman I love just went through something terrible, and if she wants to kick me out, push me away, when she's awake, then she will.

What was she doing on the road so late anyway? It was well after the time she normally came into the bar, and I try not to read too much into it. Try not to hope that she was going to visit me. It's more likely she and her grandmother had a fight and she left to blow off some steam.

Mrs. Patterson sits with a deceptive calm, her eyes closed, her hands clenched on her cane. If Rory was out on an escape, if they fought, I'm sure Mrs. Patterson is a wreck.

I sit down beside her, our thighs almost touching. *I'm here.*

Rory's leg is set and they move her into a room. Same chairs, different location. The police come in and ask us a few questions.

Mrs. Patterson explains that Rory was helping her pack, and tells them what time Rory left her apartment.

"Where was she going?" the police officer asks.

Mrs. Patterson points at me. "His bar."

I sit up.

They ask Mrs. Patterson a few more questions and then turn to me.

"What is your relation to Ms. Fox?"

"She's—she was—my fiancée."

They ask me about our breakup and the whole stupid story comes out—word vomit, really, way more than they were bargaining for. They ignore most of it.

"Where were you at the time of the accident?"

Oh god. They don't think . . .

"I was at my bar."

"Can anyone corroborate?"

"Yes," I say, with more bite than it warrants, probably. I know they're just doing their job, checking to make sure I have an alibi. "My manager was there with me, there were three customers there when I left, and we have security cameras."

They take down Hunter's information, but the whole thing leaves me feeling sick to my stomach.

But not as sick as their next question.

"Do you know anyone who would want to hurt her?"

After the cops leave, a nurse comes out to find us. "She's waking up," they say. Mrs. Patterson and I creep into the room. Rory's blinking awake, her leg suspended in a cast. "Grandma?" she asks, her voice hoarse. Her hair is a little tidier, like someone's combed through it, her road rash cleaned up, and her nose is in a splint. I notice other things I didn't see before: her right eye is swelling, the eyebrow is split; her lips are dry and slack, like maybe she's gotten a shot of Novocain.

Her eyes focus on me, and she says my name, and my heart breaks more for her when I see that something's missing—her right front tooth. Does she even know yet?

I school my face to erase the shock, but I can't stop the tears from filling my eyes. I'm so glad Mrs. Patterson called me.

Mrs. Patterson stops at Rory's bedside and gently sets a hand on her granddaughter's hair. I stand beside her and hover my hand above hers, half unsure if it would be welcome, half unsure if I can touch her without causing pain.

Rory rolls her hand palm-up, her fingers uncurling, and I slip my hand into hers. I drop my head down and close my eyes, kissing the back of her hand. It stays there when I hear Rory's sobs, and her grandmother softly comforting her.

A Battered Smile

Rory

Morgan and Grandma take turns at my bedside and I sleep away most of the day fitfully. Sometimes I wake up and Grandma's in the chair by the bed, dozing, her hands on her cane. Sometimes I wake up and it's Morgan in here with me, his head resting on our entwined fingers, while he sleeps.

I obsessively touch the hole in my gum where the tooth has gone missing. It doesn't hurt—I'm on painkillers that take care of that—but I can't stop, my tongue wanting to fill the gap in my teeth.

I have to have a consultation for a dental implant. I guess I could use this as an excuse to fix my teeth, like the dentist suggested so long ago. Maybe, when I get the implant, they can do something about the other tooth too, and I won't have this smile anymore.

Do I want that?

Morgan's soft breaths blow down the length of my forearm and I gaze down at him. I fade in and out of sleep thinking about every time Morgan called me gorgeous.

I know exactly what my ex would say, if I cared about her opinion. But I do care about Morgan's, and my heart knows that he would want whatever I want.

The police come back and talking to them wakes me up fully. I tell them about the hand brake going missing, the panic I felt when I could barely slow down in time to make the corner. Morgan squeezes my hand.

"Oh, the dashcam!" I remember.

"Yes, we recovered the SD card. Now that we know about the brakes, we'll make sure to check the footage before the incident, see if anything comes up. Is there anything else you can remember?"

I shake my head.

"I have their contact information if you think of anything," Morgan adds. He's still next to me, having woken up when the cops came in and listened to my version.

The police nod and shuffle out, leaving me, Morgan, and Grandma alone.

"Well," Grandma says, and taps her cane on the floor. She looks at me, then at Morgan, then back at me. "I think I'll wander down to the cafeteria and grab something to eat," she says, even though we ate just before the cops came.

Morgan and I are alone, and even through the drowsiness and the painkillers, I feel butterflies take up space in my stomach. He's leaning against the bed, his chin on his forearm as he looks up at me.

"How are you feeling?" he asks.

"I love you," I blurt out instead. I don't know why I'm

so nervous. Morgan has said everything except he loves me, and after reading my grandmother's emails showing his efforts to get us to stay, to make us belong *Here*, I'm pretty sure he loves me too.

But pretty sure isn't knowing.

His smile blooms, curling his lips until it's megawatt.

"That's what I was coming to tell you."

He sits up on his elbows. "Man, I wish you'd made it. It would have been the best day of my life." He wrinkles his nose. "I can't exactly say this one is, with you in the hospital and all."

"I wish I had too."

"I love you too, my queen. Of course I love you. I probably fell in love with you the first time you rolled your eyes at me."

I do it right now, and he laughs. I smile back, until I remember about my tooth.

"Don't, gorgeous," he admonishes me. "Don't worry about that now. Not when I love you so much. Because someday your teeth will fall out for other reasons and we'll have to get you dentures and I'll still fucking love you with all my heart."

My smile's back. "Surely not *all* your heart. There's gotta be room for Princess."

"And Barty. And Kit and Hunter, and, well . . . all the Herevians. And your grandmother."

I raise an eyebrow. "Really? My grandmother?"

He grins. "Even that crotchety old lady."

"I heard that!" Grandma shouts from the hallway.

Morgan straightens. "Sorry, Mrs. Patterson."

"You can call me Valerie now. Or Grandma."

Morgan's whole face brightens, pleasure radiating from him. "Okay!"

He settles back down again. "Will you move back in with me?"

I push my head back into the pillow. "Yes. But ugh, I won't be able to work for a while."

"We'll make it work."

Morgan's words have so much conviction to them. He doesn't even know how much money I have saved up or that I'll likely be able to switch to a remote office job in the meantime. "There is one thing, though," I add. "I'm not sure I want to get married. I've never really pictured myself doing the whole white dress, wedding ceremony thing. If our engagement had been real, I would have been serious about the elopement thing."

Morgan exaggerates a sigh. "I do have bad news on that front, too. I sold the ring." He grimaces. "Now I regret it . . ."

"Don't," I say. "The lodge means more to you, I know that. And also, while it was a gorgeous ring, I, uh . . . didn't like wearing it?" My voice ends on a high note, and I hope I'm not offending him.

"Oh." He blinks. His gaze shifts to the right for a moment, and then returns to me. "So, hypothetically speaking, if we did elope one day—no ceremony, just an officiant and a witness—"

There's a throat clearing from the hallway.

"Maybe a *very well-behaved octogenarian witness*," Morgan raises his voice, not that Grandma's having a hard time hearing us. "What kind of ring would you want?"

I'm grinning. It hurts. I don't care. "Well, maybe two rings—"

"*Two rings?*" he asks with mock incredulity.

"One silicone so that I can wear it while I'm working."

"Smart."

"And one small band."

"No diamond?"

"No diamond," I confirm.

"Gold? Silver? Platinum?"

"Gold," I decide. "Maybe engraved?"

"Romantic."

"Shut up."

"Make me."

One little tug is all it takes, and Morgan rises up to gently kiss my battered—but happy—smile.

Here Is Home

MORGAN

PRINCESS IS POGOING AGAIN.

Boing.

I park my truck in the driveway right up by the garage.

Boing.

I get out and wave at Mrs. Patterson on the back porch. She gets to her feet while I walk around to the passenger side.

Boing.

I bend down. "All right, my queen, ready to come home?"

Rory tosses her head back against the headrest. "Yesssssss."

It's a hell of a lot easier for me to scoop Rory out of the truck than it is for her to get out on her own accord, so I dig my arms underneath her legs, careful of the cast, and pull her out of the car. My live-in girlfriend (yesssssss!!!!) wraps her arms around my neck. Mrs. Patterson waits at the gate.

Boing.

"Good heavens," Rory's grandmother tells my dog. "Get ahold of yourself, young lady."

I stop at the fence and Rory reaches a hand down to Princess. The pogoing stops and the energy is converted to a full-body wiggle instead. Then, just like I expected, Princess darts off to find a toy to bring to Rory.

My dog isn't the only one excited to have her home. Things have been a hectic mess around here, but a beautiful hectic mess.

The day after Rory talked to the police, I was at work —Rory's grandma was with her—when my phone blew up. My mom. Over and over. I couldn't ignore it, so I answered and I'll probably regret that for the rest of my life. I don't like to think about the awful things my mom said to me, blaming me for my brother's arrest.

While the dashcam from Rory's motorcycle couldn't get a plate number in the dark at the time that she was hit, it did get a good look at my brother's face when he sabotaged her bike. And while he did a pretty good job of hiding the evidence of the hit-and-run on his truck, he didn't count on the cops showing up with a search warrant and finding a few pounds of meth in his garage.

I still can't believe my brother was so angry—and greedy—over something as stupid as selling us a car that had the *potential* to be worth so much more. I have always been more forgiving of people than Graham ever was, but for him to hold on so violently still surprised me.

I finally did the thing I should have done years ago—I blocked my mom. I blocked my brother too, even though it probably doesn't matter. He's going to prison for a long time for possession with intent to distribute and attempted manslaughter.

Princess can't decide which toy to bring to Rory—she grabs one, makes it a few steps, then changes her mind and drops it for another, then repeats the whole thing again and again—giving us time to get Rory into the house and settled on the couch. Barty meows indignantly when we gently shove him off to make room and he runs off to hide.

Yes, he's back living with me, too. I missed my little loaf.

Mrs. Patterson sits in the chair while I shift some pillows around and just generally fuss over my *live-in girlfriend* (again: yesssss!!!!) and Rory lounges like royalty.

She grins up at me. "I could get used to you fluffing my pillows."

Mrs. Patterson snorts.

Rory's grin is back, even though the tooth is still missing. She scheduled an implant and wants her new tooth to look just like her old one.

Rory's hungry, so I make us all sandwiches. I perch on the coffee table in front of Rory while I eat mine, and we chitchat until Mrs. Patterson interrupts us.

"Morgan. In the hospital you said that you sold the ring?"

"You mean when you were eavesdropping?" I grin at her.

She ignores me. "Rory said the lodge was more important. What did that mean?"

I tell Mrs. Patterson about how the lodge is up for sale and my friends and I are all chipping in to try to buy it.

Mrs. Patterson looks at Rory. "Perhaps you should cash that check. It's no strings attached, remember? You could chip in."

Rory opens her mouth, stops, and then closes it.

"You're committing to this one." Mrs. Patterson jerks her thumb at me. "I think you should commit to Here, too."

Rory looks at me. "Would that be weird for you? To have your girlfriend be a business partner?"

I shrug. "Bailey and Silas are doing it. I would love for you to be involved."

"I don't even ski," she says, as if that would stop her from being part owner in a ski lodge.

"You don't ski *yet*. And you probably won't this season." I gesture at her leg. "But next year I'll teach you. Or you can always stick to après-ski and come hang out with me in the bar."

Mrs. Patterson finishes her sandwich and sets the plate on the table before picking her cane up and resting both hands on it. "Would your friends be interested in a silent investor?"

My eyebrows rise. "You?"

She snorts. "No, Barty. *Of course*, me. I would be interested in contributing, but I don't want all that messiness that comes with it. I'd match Rory's buy-in."

I pull out my phone. "Let me see if Hunter's free to come by sometime and chat with you. He knows way more than I do." I send a message to him and then take Rory's empty plate and set it on the table.

Last weekend, in preparation for Rory coming back home, my friends and I hosted Sunday Funday at Rory's apartment, without her. We loaded up on breakfast burritos from a place Rory recommended and when we'd finished eating we played a round of Whose Turn Is It Anyway? Rory's prize for the winner was a promise of being the first person (aside from Rory or me) to get a ride in the Bronco when it was done being rebuilt. Jared and Tuan fought hard for it, but Bailey won.

After that was done, we packed up Rory's apartment—furniture and all—and moved her out. We caravanned back to Here and unpacked in my house, which is why the guest bedroom is stuffed full of boxes and furniture. Now that Rory's home, we can decide what stuff to sell and what to keep.

Mrs. Patterson has opinions on some of the furniture pieces, and we wander into the guest bedroom to discuss where to put an old wood card table, which apparently belonged to Rory's mother. It needs refinishing, but Rory wants to keep it, so Mrs. Patterson and I discuss which of my less-sentimental pieces to get rid of.

When I glance at the couch next, Rory's asleep. Princess is carefully wedged in her usual spot between Rory and the back of the couch.

"I should take you home," I whisper to Mrs. Patterson.

She pats my arm. "Here is home. Welcome to the family, Morgan."

Red Carpet

MORGAN, *A FEW WEEKS LATER*

Sunday Funday has a notable absence this week—Kit.

"Where is he?" Hunter asks, looking worried.

The rest of us exchange glances. We're at Hunter's house, because it's too cold up on the mountain to play. So far it's just the eight of us.

Hunter's got a card table set up next to his dining room table to fit enough seats for everyone and we've plunked Rory there with her cast. She's grumpy because she's on painkillers and can't have a mimosa (which Bailey has decorated with fanned-out strawberry slices and I would love to see Rory enjoying one).

Bailey's half a drink in already and has been complaining about some tax kerfuffle at her job to Leo, who sits next to her looking confused and saying things like, "I thought taxes were due April fifteenth" and "But why would you prepay taxes?" Silas sits next to her. Jared and Quinn round out the group. Tuan had a family obligation, so at least we know where he is.

But Kit . . . he's a no-call, no-show.

"When was the last time Kit missed Sunday Funday?" Leo asks.

Hunter's arms are crossed over his chest and he's peering out the front window. "Not since he moved back from Albany."

"Maybe he's with—" I snap my mouth shut, having just remembered that I'm not *supposed* to know that he's been spending time with a certain celebrity.

Hunter's eyes narrow. "With who?"

Fortunately Silas interrupts. "Come on, you've seen him around town a few times with that woman, Jess."

"Yeah, but still. He wouldn't miss Sunday Funday."

"Should we start without him?" Bailey asks.

Hunter doesn't answer for a moment, and then he sighs. "Let's give it five more minutes." He paces over to the table and picks up his phone. "I wish he was answering our texts."

Bailey and Silas exchange glances over their mimosas and Hunter resumes pacing.

"So, you have a kid?" Rory asks Jared, who is more than happy to tell my girlfriend how "fucking cool" his daughter is.

After the five minutes are up, we start our game without Kit. We're a few rounds in and I've just given Hunter a penalty for playing out of turn (on an easy move, but he's so distracted he can't function properly) when Bailey's phone buzzes.

She picks it up, frowning at the screen, and taps something. Her eyes widen.

"Oh my god. Kit's in LA."

Hunter stands. "What do you mean Kit's in LA?"

Bailey holds her phone out and presses the button to turn up the volume. She leans over to show the video to Rory and the rest of us gather around.

The video is of a red-carpet event with a woman's

torso superimposed over it. She's pointing up, her finger poking the face of someone in a tuxedo.

Not *someone*. Kit. He's standing next to Julie Meyer—yes, *the* Julie Meyer, and I wonder if my NDA is valid anymore—who is dressed like a hot vampire—right out of Anne Rice, I swear to god—and she has her hand on the back of his neck while they look at each other.

Her voice gets louder. ". . . who the fuck is this guy? No one knows. But after he did this move here—"

I watch on the screen in slo-mo as Kit says something that looks like "well . . ." and takes her hand from the back of his neck, twines his fingers through hers, and presses a kiss to her pulse point.

But it's not just a kiss.

"Look at that!" the woman in the video shouts. I can only see from her eyes up now, and that accusatory finger pointing at my best friend. "Look at that! I'm pregnant just from that eye contact. That is a man who knows he's gonna—*bleep*—the hell out of her tonight."

"Holy fucking shit," Jared says.

We watch the video again. Yeah, Kit's eyes are hot on Julie's, his lips soft on her wrist, and there's a flash of teeth against her skin.

A third time. Julie's eyes darken, her lips part.

I've seen Kit flirt with plenty of women. This is something different.

"Did you know he was in LA?" Hunter asks, though I'm not sure who he's asking.

"He's never even been on an airplane before," I murmur.

"How does he know . . ." Silas trails off. "Oh my god, Jess."

Everyone groans but me and Leo.

Leo looks around. "What? Do you think he's cheating on Jess?"

"No," Bailey explains. "Jess *is* Julie."

Hunter's head whips over to me. "Did you know that?"

"Uh . . ." I hate lying to Hunter, but I do *not* want to get sued, not when I've just gotten the money to buy into the lodge.

Silas saves the day. "How did you find this?" he asks Bailey.

"Remember my college roommate Becky who came for Thanksgiving one year? She sent it to me."

"How does she know who Kit is?" Jared asks.

Bailey rolls her eyes. "Guess."

They boinked. Kit and I both thought she was hot and had a friendly competition. He won.

"If she figured out who Kit is, other people will," Hunter says. "Everyone is going to know that she's been here. She might be coming back. People will be talking in town, on social media. Maybe there will even be paparazzi."

The last word hangs in the air, but it feels like it carries the weight of impending doom.

This is going to be a shit show.

This was probably the most fun I ever had writing a book. I hope it showed.

I would not have gotten this book written without Felicia Davin, who I met with once or twice a week at our amazing local library to work on our stories. Shout-out to libraries and librarians!

Thank you to my early readers, Lainey Davis, Payson, and Serena Bell.

Thank you to my proofreader, Dan Janeck, and to Marten Noor for the cutest character art.

And as always, a big thank-you to my husband, who encouraged me so much from day one, and my parents, all five of them, who supported this book in one way or another.

Liz Alden used to live on a sailboat with her husband. Now she's in her small town era and living in Western Mass.

She knows exactly how big the world is—having sailed around it—and exactly how small it is, having bumped into friends worldwide.

She's been a dishwasher, an engineer, a CEO, and occasionally gets paid to write or sail.

The books are inspired by her real-life travel.

Follow Liz: